AYDIN

AYDIN
An Admiral Press book
First edition 2020

This is a work of fiction and the characters portrayed in it are fictional
and used in a fictitious manner. Any resemblance to actual persons,
living or dead, is coincidental. The actions and events in it did not
happen and are products of the author's imagination.

Cover: Jana Jelovac
Editor: Neil Danby
This book is typeset in Garamond

Admiral Press
Cape Town, South Africa
info@admiralpress.org

ISBN: 978-0-620-88155-5

For Mounir

PART I

1

I'm running up an echoing stairwell. It smells of concrete. Dusty spider recess windows look out on a courtyard frowned on by tall, dirty tenements thrown up quickly after a war when Berlin was made rubble – thrown up by my Turkish father and others like him who carried the beams and shovelled the sand and poured the pitted concrete steps I'm running up, panting, my heart sore, four flights, past unmarked red metal doors.

I reach the gym door where I know what to do. I open it and go along the passage, past the changing rooms full of naked, barking, braying men. A bodybuilder is behind the bar serving protein drinks, chatting up girls loudly, sunbed-brown, sky-blue eyes too intense; I can't look; he grins in his pock-marked pumpkin face. We pretend to like each other. I hurry through the carpeted weights area. The carpet here is old and red. There's the muscular girl; don't know her name; she's not young. She's tall, blonde and frightening. Veins, leathery skin, threadbare leotard, tantalising, repellent, making me look.

Past the weight racks and machines, everywhere mirrors trying to catch my eye. I don't mind mirrors, but in here they make me look thin and wiry among the steroid hulks. I pass along some windows with venetian blinds, just in time, the Master's going through the flimsy plywood door just up ahead, a frayed, faded black belt dangling gently from an overhanging belly wrapped in a thick, stiff, white gi. I slip in through the door before he closes it.

He looks at me with nut-brown eyes. "Aydin Mesüt, you're late: thirty push-ups – on wood."

I relish his punishments because he watches me. My knuckles go down onto the wooden strip that borders the red mat. Others look on nervously in quickly formed ranks. Ten. The Master paces the ranks, saying nothing. I see only his small, smooth, tanned feet pass by the left of my head.

"Eyes ahead."

Twenty. I'm feeling strong. I want to show him. I want him to admire me. My knuckles settle into the hard wood. In the first year they hurt and I shifted them around, making it worse. The second year they hurt and I ignored it. Now they're deadened, flattened, they sit nicely on the wood. They have been adapted for hitting. I hear an object being taken down from the far wall. The only other sound in this room is my breathing.

Thirty. I jump up and go straight to my place centre-front. Only one person has a better place than me, at the front-right but I don't begrudge him that. He's a muscleman, but not like the ones outside who strut among the weights. Mario. Of all the bodybuilders who ever peered in through those venetian blinds, he's the only one who came through the door and stayed, didn't slink back to the machines after feeling what gets dealt out in here. Mario. Bronze, could be mixed-race, a determined, blue-eyed gaze, chiselled jaw, knows everyone. They say he's a junior bodybuilding champion but I've never asked him. We pretend not to be interested in each other. As an emblem of manhood he's perfect. The body. The face. The social skills.

Training starts and doesn't stop. It's "ten," it's "left, right," it's "on your backs," it's "jack-knives" until one by one the jack-knives fold up in moans of pain. The Master paces the ranks, gently swinging a heavy wood-en pole. Then he stops, facing a newcomer.

"All lie down. Tense your stomachs."

The newcomer obeys. We all obey. He becomes a terrified plank but the Master only pats him on the abdomen with the pole then moves on. One of the things I admire about the Master is he has no rules; he does as his mood takes him.

"Tense your stomach." The next student, a woman, gets a harder pat, almost a slap, but the Master doesn't hit girls hard.

"Tense your stomach." The next person gets a proper thwack.

"Good. Next. Tense your stomach…"

He's moving at random now. Thwack. That one must have hurt.

"Good. Tense your stomach…"

Then he walks down the back row, standing on each stomach: no heavy wooden pole for the white-belts.

We in the front row always get left for last.

"Raoul, tense your stomach. Ready?" Raoul's on my left, a big, strong man of around twenty who speaks German in a way that runs rings around me. I lie there, my feet still raised, containing my fear as I've learned to do.

"Ready?" He's asking Raoul twice, which could mean something bad. Then a loud thumping into meat, followed by another. Raoul's wind is blown out of him but he's keeping it together. Someone at the back says something under his breath; the Master glances up.

Then he approaches me and I catch his eye, but he passes me. Mario is next. Without warning the Master swings his thick wooden staff so fast it makes the air whoosh. Mario roars in defiance. Thud – and the roar is silenced. Someone at the back gets up, bows to the dojo and leaves without a word.

Mario retches and groans, curling up sideways like a crushed caterpillar, his eyes screwed shut in agony; the Master nods at him, which is a compliment. Now it's my turn. The Master looks down at me and chuckles. You can never tell what it means. He stands over me, tests my abdomen with the edge of his chopping foot and steps back. He swings the pole from right behind him in a big blurring arc and shouts – screams – as the heavy lump of wood comes down.

Later in the session, when our stiff white suits have become drenched, grey and soft, we don red and blue boxing gloves and foam pads that strap around the bottom of our shins and feet. I wish we used them more. We're paired off for two-minute bouts. First I fight a beginner and let him take some shots, just guarding my head. I let him kick me, land some punches, then test him with a few shots. I feel protective of him. After that I'm watching other bouts. It goes on and on. All I want to do is fight someone good.

Eventually I'm paired with Lars, the doctor. He's wiry like me and I can't hurt him so I don't let him see he's hurting me. We dance around and around, glaring at each other and exchanging shots: kicks to the stomach and legs, punches to the chest, arms and face. Fending them off hurts almost more than the ones he lands. After an age it finishes; no one wins.

Then it's just Mario and me left: we re-tighten our foot-guards, face off, everyone's watching and wondering in the hot evening. The Master closes the one remaining open window. Condensation is forming on the panes. I glance at the venetian blinds and spot some huge silhouettes, observing us between the slats.

"Ajamé."

Mario wastes no time and comes straight in aiming his shin at my lower thigh, too fast, too strong. I move back, then he tries again and again, low-kick after low-kick. I can't get near him: I'm frightened of that shin and his animal power. His neck is twice the thickness of mine, his forearms huge and perfectly formed, layer on layer of muscles tight beneath his bronze, hairless skin. We circle and circle and he keeps trying to kick me but I stay just out of range.

The Master breaks us up and takes me aside.

"Aydin," he says to me, lowering his voice and turning his back on Mario. "If he's going to do the same move every time then make him pay. Present your left leg," he whispers, "but don't move back, just lift your foot off the floor. Then move forward and you've got him." The Master's nut-brown eyes drill me.

Within the space of three seconds it happens just like he said. I present my leg, Mario kicks with all his might, shouting, I lift my foot from the floor, he swings right through, catching my foot harmlessly, so I punch him straight in the face, knocking his head unnaturally far back and sending spray all over the mats. The onlookers moan. One even turns away.

Mario recovers though. There is some blood around his lapels and sleeves. Later on in those never-ending two minutes he gets me back by winding me and filling me with rage and humiliation. I almost cry but I manage not to.

The Master owns the gym and he owns the dojo, it's all his place. He seems to own everything. Inside the dojo he's urging, drilling, teaching, correcting, chiding, shouting, encouraging; but outside among the weights and at the protein bar he's aloof, pacing slowly, flexing his fingers, swinging his arms and his torso, looking straight ahead, his big belly leading the way, oriental flat-foot, a horse's tail of thick black hair hanging behind, gesturing to this one, greeting that one but never talking much. Everyone's in awe of him. At the entrance there are some photos of him as a young, mixed-race man smashing piles of bricks, another of him sitting on a chair surrounded by proud-looking young students, standing to attention. Once I asked and they told me he'd won the German full-contact karate championships for thirteen consecutive years. That's all I know.

There's a woman who works behind the protein bar who I think is his. She's more familiar with him than anyone else and less polite to him; she sometimes gives him daggers. She would have been pretty once. She looks like she might never be happy. I don't dare talk to her.

After training's over I'm on my way out, passing

the protein bar where some bodybuilders are gathered, horsing around and laughing darkly. The Master is there with someone and he says to me, "Aydin."

"Yes?"

"I like the way you fight."

I don't know how to reply. In three years I've never heard him praise me or anyone else. So I just say thanks and walk off.

I'm running down the concrete stairwell, three at a time clattering in the echo chamber, feeling high, high, king of the world. The Master never, ever pays people compliments. I'm the only one he praised, because I smashed Mario who everyone thought was the best. I'm out in the courtyard. There's the Master's car with tinted windows, compact, fast, powerful and dangerous, its inside hidden from the outside world. I want to be like that. I want to be like him so people look at me like they look at him, so people gather around me like they gather around him, so people fear me like they fear him. He must have money too. Endless money. He must live a life where you choose the things you want.

Out in the warm street I'm thirsty. Normally I buy a drink at the protein bar, but the bodybuilders scared me off so I didn't. My mouth and throat are so dry. It's is the excuse I was looking for. I've promised myself only to drink on Fridays and Saturdays – except if there's a reason, and this is a reason. I'm going for a real drink.

The sky above is darkening to a clear, melancholy blue and a bird silhouette crosses from one building to another, settling down for the night in one of the plane trees that line all the roads here. Sensible bird. I quicken and cross the road, dodging a car which beeps in the warm evening. I'm going down a side street and out onto the big avenue where an old couple laden with shopping bags are waiting to cross, although there's no traffic. I wait by them, obeying the red man for their sake; I don't like to worry elderly German people; besides, they might scold me and hate me. But they are studiously not looking at me; the sides of their faces don't move a muscle when I turn my head to acknowledge them. Maybe they're afraid like I am; to them I am a foreign man in their sullen island city which our fathers helped rebuild. I look away.

Why won't they cross this empty avenue? When they finally move, there is a flip and a plastic rustle and a bouncing of onions all over the pavement and road.

"Oh," she exclaims, stooping shakily.

"Ah, mind out, the shopping's spilled," he says, bending stiffly down to help. I crouch to help too and he glances at me in fear. We pick up canned fish and vegetables.

Then someone appears from nowhere and pushes her over and grabs something; she collapses onto the road and a man in a brown jacket is running away and now a car comes and squeals its tyres and thuds right into her as it stops, knocking her with its plastic bumper from one sitting position to another, but she only cries out in a shrill angry voice: "My handbag! He's taken my handbag!"

Her husband's got her in his arms and they're both stuttering, gibbering and terrified, so I'm off down the street, I'm going after the brown jacket and the handbag. I will show those two old West Berliners what this strange young foreign man can do for them in their sullen island city.

Shouts come from around and about, echoing among the hot buildings; people aren't stupid. I'm running fast and these are my Berlin streets where I run so what are you thinking, running man? His back is getting bigger already, his brown leather jacket billowing like mine, the handbag flailing in his hand. He turns his head as he approaches a side street and I see his moustache and his Turkish features like my uncle's. He has to wait for two cars which he tries to go around. Frightened-horse eyes meet mine just for a second then he's off but he's huffing and puffing and I don't mind cars so I just sprint across between screeching brakes and blaring horns and he's in reach now – so how does he think this is going to end? He's slowing up, he's beat, just a lowlife thief with no training, he's turning to face me now and there's a knife out but I love the closure, I live for the embrace. I dive headlong and hit him on the fly, I tackle him in half and cut him down and we're on the pavement – the hard pavement and its grit – and stones grind into my hand and knees but there's no pain.

"Fuck you."

"Fuck you," then I hit him hard and it's much better without boxing gloves because something always snaps in their faces. He jabs at my face with the blade and jerks madly under my weight, eyes like a terrified dog at the slaughter and I punch his head down, making his skull hit the paving slab. I'm up on my feet now over him and he tries one more time feebly with the knife but misses my leg and I lift my foot ready to stamp his head, when someone, another Turk, pulls me back. "That's enough, brother. You've done it. You've done it."

I push the intervener away, pick up the handbag and walk off, lungs heaving, heart pounding, back towards the old couple streets away. People, mostly Turks, are standing in shop doors looking at me in the warm evening. One man says something admiring to me but I don't look. Two brown children come alongside and skip and point and ogle and giggle and disappear. But I don't need praise now.

The old woman is hugging her shoulder, sitting propped against the post that holds up the green man they were waiting for. Pacing up and down and smoking, fear in his face, is the driver of the car that hit her. Tears are streaming all over her wrinkly face; I don't like to see that. You shouldn't see old people crying, especially old Germans who are never supposed to cry. Her husband is comforting her – so awkwardly, even after all these years. She's ignoring him and looking up at me, holding out her hands, into which I place the handbag.

"Thank you, thank you. Such a fine young man, a fine young man."

The husband turns fearfully to look at me.

"Yes, thank you," he adds in a trembling voice, surrounded by onions and tissues, tin cans and plastic bags, their orderly Berlin life spewed out on the pavement. "Wait," and he takes the handbag from his trembling wife. "We'd withdrawn our savings today. Here's something for you," and he hands me a hundred marks but I shrink away. That is not what I did it for.

"No thanks."

They stare at me.

"No thanks. Thank you."

I don't know how to talk to elderly German people so I move away and cross at the red man, thinking how that might turn them against me.

"Mind the traffic, you shouldn't cross," calls the man, but his voice is not harsh, it's concerned.

"Your face is cut," calls his wife in a strong sorry voice, and as I decipher her words I feel a burning coming on in my cheek and something sticky there too but I don't look back. I look at my hands instead. The skin is off on the outside edges of my palms and now my elbow stings with a pulse that shoots up my arm to my neck. I move it and it works.

I'm checking my gi now beneath my leather jacket and there are spots and streaks of blood. To hell with it. I spit out some blood and push on up the road: now I really have licence to drink. Café Abgang is coming into sight and the two old green tables with benches are outside which means it's summer and there's my friend Slobodan, waiting for no one and smoking alone. My heart skips and I laugh when I see him.

When he sees me coming, his watery blue blood-shot eyes light up and his cigarette perks up in his bulgy, stubbly face, but when he sees my cuts his face hardens and the cigarette almost falls out.

"Shit. What happened with you? You been fighting?"

"Yep."

"That's a bad cut – ugh. I can see your teeth through that hole, that's disgusting." He winces and taps his ash on the pavement.

"So what. Can I roll myself one?"

He looks away and hands me a navy blue packet. I lean in through the door of the pub. Jürgen the land-lord is behind the bar. I order a beer then change my mind and order a korn instead. Slobodan is watching me.

"Korn? Seeing the parents after, are we?"

"Might do."

We settle down to talk, me with a paper napkin

to my throbbing face and I tell him what happened. Slobodan is Serbian. Unlike me, he speaks practically perfect German – except when he's angry. It's ironic, since he only came here as an adult whereas I was born here. But my parents kept me away from Germans. I only had Turkish friends when I was small. Slobo's still an outsider though, a piece of gristle in this Berlin stew. He told me he was in the Serbian army before he came here, and he came because of something he did, but he never told me what it was and I never feel I can ask. It's as if something dark hangs over his past. He's handsome in his way, with his strong jaw and blue eyes, but he has no girl. I went to his flat once. There was a dirty bulldog there curled up in a sloppy beanbag that no one had washed. Fleas were in it. The bulldog was wearing a harness labelled "couch potato" and its face was pressed in like an injury, revealing rotten lower teeth. It got to its feet slowly and welcomed me with a wet sneeze. There were topless magazines and ashtrays strewn around the flat, and the washing up was not done. There was a dartboard with holes in the wall around it. There was a fishbowl with no fish, just algae. I love Slobodan but I'm worried for him, the way he lives, and because of the dark thing in his past. On the shelves where his television and record collection are, there is a framed picture of him in fatigues, his army friends on either side; he looks much younger and healthier. He has a cigarette dangling from his mouth, even then. They are holding rifles with pride. Maybe

Slobodan killed some Muslims in his time, and that's why he doesn't talk about it with me.

The clear glassy spirits of the korn burn in my cheek like fire. But it's better than beer because it doesn't make your breath smell. After two drinks Slobodan persuades me to go with him to hospital. We pay the tab and stroll to his big, dusty old Merc, crammed in a side street between other cars and plastered with bird droppings. He always drives, however drunk he gets, never takes the U-Bahn. He says the U-Bahn's depressing.

We sit in a shiny hospital corridor beneath strip lights. An hour passes, then they come and take me to a room and sew my cheek shut with green thread, leaving ugly trimmed ends poking out from clotted blood. Then we drive back to Abgang, park in the same spot, and drink some more. It feels wrong to go back to the same pub in one evening. I abandon caution and the odourless liquor and start knocking back beers that dizzy my empty stomach and the world begins to spin in numbness and floating joy. And everyone knows all there is to know.

We play pinball, getting scores in the millions, losing track of time and fearlessly feeding coins into the slot. Then Slobodan produces a tiny folded-up piece of paper the size of a razor blade.

"Here, wipe some of this on your cut."

I go to the toilet, unfold the sachet on top of the toilet lid, kneel amid the urine puddles and dab some

of the white powder inside my mouth, feeling the alien
stitch-thread with my fingertip, then I roll up a bank-
note, sniff up the rest of the powder and go back out,
punch-numb in the nose and face, seeing icy shooting stars and everyone looking at me and I understand
everything even more and I love everything and can
flip the flippers even faster than Slobo and all the
heaviness of the world is gone.

Paying my bar-tab at the end does dent me, but money
has to get spent on something, and given the way I
earn it, it may as well be this. I wander home through
familiar streets with my ears ringing and a faint blue
morning throwing out black patterns of leaves and tall
buildings above. West Berlin. It doesn't change; it's as
if it's been like this for ever, which is strange really, as
it was blown to pieces in the war. But they rebuilt it so
fast. Then they put the Wall up and West Berlin just sat
down and stopped, no ambition and no anxiety. Things
are comfortable here. Everyone has work, there's plen-
ty of money, and because you're surrounded by a wall
with landmines, you can't really go anywhere except
for day-trips into the East German wasteland, so you
just accept things as they are, a sombre, comfortable
patch in a socialist sea, with big parks, an urban organ-
ism that's dozed – until now. Now, the Wall's opened
and everyone's on tenterhooks as droves of Easterners stream in.

Actually, the Wall is mostly still there; they haven't removed it yet. If you go down our street and turn right then left, it's suddenly there in front of you, a big, dark bulwark with a rounded top, like reaching the end of the world. Beyond you can see the tops of buildings in East Berlin, but you don't ever see many people.

Birds are singing a dawn rapture and a big one flies across the open piece of sky from one side of the street to the other. I'm home and I feel drunk and a bit sick. Quietly now: just don't wake them, softly on silent feet in the carpet corridor. The toilet flushes and I get a fright; my father must be up for the dawn prayer, the opposite of my drunken nights. I close my door behind me with a click just as the bathroom door opens. There is a long silence and I hear my thumping heart, then carpeted footsteps recede.

My bedroom is silent, my bed unmade. My pillow doesn't smell good. And I have work in three hours. The alarm clock says 03:58 and the double-dots are flashing fast. I set the alarm to 05:47 and turn it away so I can't see the dreaded numbers. Then I turn it back and it says 04:01. I want to smash the clock; I reset the alarm to 06:07. I need sleep more than breakfast.

Next thing I know, everyone is crying – even my father. I ask them why but they won't answer. Then there's a police siren chasing me and I'm running and it's catching me up in the dark of the night beneath city lights and it's almost upon me and I go down under the front wheels and the siren bleats and I cry out and sit bolt upright. My alarm clock is screaming and my brain is dislodged. I'm feeling sick and want to vomit and the room rotates and curves; sickly sunlight slants in. I close my curtain and slump back on the smelly pillow and wonder what to do.

I'm in a damp cellar, then I'm with some women on a beach and I get excited but because it's a dream, I needn't feel ashamed – who's there to laugh at you when it's a dream? Then there's a dark sea swirling like a vast pit of stirred, searing oil. I'm sweating and I don't know why. Then one of the women is my mother.

"Aydin."

"Aydin."

Her plaintive voice comes from somewhere.

"Aydin, wake up," says her muffled voice from another room. "You've slept in."

I jolt and turn my clock round to see 07:59. How did it get to that number? Work started an hour ago. I hear my mother hesitating on the carpet outside my door.

I shout at her: "Leave me alone please."

I'm throwing off the bedclothes, opening the door and pushing past her faltering, headscarfed frame into the bathroom: it's urgent because I don't want to vomit anywhere except in the toilet.

Her plaintive voice persists behind me and turns gradually accusative. "What's wrong with your face?

Where have you been?"

I slam the bathroom door without replying, lock it, and hug the bleachy toilet bowl and retch, but nothing comes out.

I'm running to work, not taking the underground. Maybe then I'll sweat out some of what's in my veins. Besides, if I really run, it's quicker than the U-Bahn. When I finally get there, panting, down in the bowels of the department store, Ezra is waiting for me. His eyes are bloodshot.

"Why you not come? Why you make me wait?"

He prods me hard in the chest. Ezra is from Ghana. His shaved, mahogany head comes up to my chin. He always knows what he's doing.

"Why I cover for you, drinking the night away?" Then he wrinkles his nose and takes a step back. "You smell bad, brother."

I can't look him in the face. Then I force myself to, and I apologise. He huffs and goes off and clocks out with a ching, waving and smiling to the organised, reliable German men behind the glass panel who eye me with disgust, conferring with each other. Ezra begins to walk along the concrete loading bay but looks over his shoulder, checking out my stitched face before turning away and disappearing around the corner.

I go straight to the rubbish press. Trolleys and trolleys of stuff are lined up waiting to be crushed. Ezra stayed late for me but he didn't do my work. I'm setting about it now, taking out polystyrene trays of old food. There are peaches, mostly mouldy. One still looks alright so I pocket it for later and throw the rest into the mouth of the machine; but then I throw the good one in too so it can join its companions. The machine has metallic, oily, rotting breath. All sorts of debris is stuck to its inside, where the huge steel surfaces shear across each other: tabloid newspaper shreds, smears of decayed food, hair, oil. I take more trays out of the next trolley, these ones containing lots of identical little fluffy toy chicks staring up in petrified ranks. Why? I force myself to throw them in. Then lots of empty polystyrene pieces in inexplicable shapes. It all goes in. Next trolley, full of more unsold, unwanted things – I throw them in. Such a waste. Then the trolley from the fishmonger. I pull out a tray and some pungent fish-liquid slops down my front. Cursing and curious, I open the lid of the tray. Inside is a deep-sea type of fish, black and slimy, with a jellylike antenna that has fallen aside and skewed eyes that point up at different angles, the whole thing swaying in foul black water. Who would eat that? Its black eyes look up at me maddeningly so I throw it into the machine and press the green mushroom button which starts the crushing, all and everything, shunting it back with terrifying force into a ribbed steel truck trailer docked onto the end. Three more trolleys then I can move to the cardboard press. Cleaner and drier, it produces satisfying cuboid bales of board which drop off the end, then I get to use the forklift to carry them away.

This is the job I do. I found it in the papers, just to show my parents I could work and get money that doesn't come from them, because, even though they always gave me just enough money, they made me feel guilty for not working and they always compared me with my older brother Ahmet. Even now they still do. He's so different from me. He works at my father's company and makes big money, but I never wanted to. I didn't know what I wanted to do, I just knew what I didn't want. I wouldn't have minded doing nothing, but they never let the subject drop, it was always waiting in the air and anything would get them started on what I was going to do with my life, how I was wasting my time. Now they don't do that, but I know they're still unhappy. And I know they know I go drinking, but they can't prove it so they can't say anything; I'll just deny it.

The boss, a short, overalled man with grey hair, is coming along the loading bay with a woman from upstairs in cosmetics. All the women upstairs wear make-up, but the ones from cosmetics wear the most. I've never been up there, except to the canteen on floor five; but a lot of them come down here. He chats and chats with her, smiling, his eyes mostly on her face but also taking in her pretty chest. He's twice her age at least. The two of them are coming closer. Then he glances at me and sees the trolleys, and his smile fades.

"Aydin, what's this? What are all these still doing here? Come on."

The woman doesn't look at me, she stands facing sideways, her lovely shape at odds with this tarred, angular, concrete bay and its dirty machines. I want her to look at me but I don't, what with my fish stain and stitched cheek. I'm lucky today: the boss usually comes at eight, not nine. He would have fired me.

"There's so much today, sorry," I say.

He huffs and turns to the woman. "Just give that to him," he says, gesturing at a black bin-bag she's holding, and she hands me it while looking carefully at a spot somewhere behind me.

The shift has ended now and I'm feeling better, just a rumbling stomach and a low-grade headache. I'm walking back home down the busy, sunny afternoon boulevard between grey and brown buildings, some older and ornate from before the war, some plain and grey, built quickly afterwards by honest, hard-working men like my father. I'm enjoying the wide pavement and looking into passing shops that sell musical instruments, doner kebabs, second-hand cameras, package holidays and groceries. There's no karate today – and definitely no drinking. Must keep away from drinking in the week. I stop at a chemist to buy aspirins and a plaster for the stitches.

Back at our flat I'm hanging up my jacket on a peg

in the corridor but what's that on a hook next to mine? A long, grey tunic made of nylon with many fabric-covered grey buttons right down the front. It's Imam Osman's coat. He always wears it and it's always clean and never creased. It has shoulder-pads and static that makes my arm hairs stand on end if I brush against it. I quickly make for my bedroom but it's too late, out of the lounge comes my father.

"Aydin."

He means come and I obey, unable not to. Come and have tea he means, tea with the Imam. Come and listen to what you have to do, what you have to not do, and what awaits someone in Hell for drinking and fornicating. They have no idea I'm a virgin.

Imam Osman Dermitaş is sitting there on the sofa facing me, his feet and knees together, his hands folded. He must have learned that pose somewhere. He's got grey hair, a tiny, neat, grey moustache, colourless skin. His turban is made of white synthetic material, hard like plastic.

I walk over to shake his hand. It's limp and cold like the fish I crushed earlier. He doesn't look at me, he averts his eyes and says carefully and smoothly: "As-salaamu alaykum."

"Guten Tag Imam Osman," I reply, even though he doesn't speak German.

"That's no way to greet," says mother from the side, but I ignore her and plump down onto the other sofa and scan for biscuits.

The Imam looks over to the window, his hands still folded.

He begins to speak, beginning with "Your father and mother asked me to drop in," but what he is saying soon after that, I cannot tell, I can't fix my mind on it and my stomach is still upset from last night. My head throbs. Father is there listening and nodding. His hair is also grey but more silver than the Imam's and he has finer features, a beautiful nose. I glance to see it then look away. My mother is wrapped in her permanent headscarf, wringing her hands. When did she start looking so old?

At the end of the tea I say yes I will follow the Imam's advice. I go to my room, put on earphones and my Walkman, and sleep.

I'm running up the concrete stairwell to the gym where I know what to do. Inside on the red mat a senior black belt who rarely attends is standing at the front where the Master belongs. It's not the same without the Master and, to my mind, this man hasn't earned the right to teach us, especially as he comes so seldom. I go through the motions, work up a sweat, practice the moves. Then we all pair up; I'm with Lars who doesn't show pain. We have to kick each other's thighs again and again in the exact same spot. My shin hurts when I kick him and when he kicks me my thigh hurts but he just stares back so I stare back. I think we actually like each other underneath. I definitely respect him. There must be more to him than meets the eye.

Then we kick the pads held up high. He's good at it and so am I. We work up a rhythm of smacking until everyone's watching, even the black-belt teacher. I wish the Master was here to stop us showing off.

Afterwards at the protein bar I'm drinking my protein when in walks the Master wearing jeans and a dark blue shirt, collar wide open revealing a golden chain on his tanned, hairless chest, cuffs folded back over thick wrists. His eyes take in everything and he spots me.

"Aydin," he barks. He walks over, making a show of looking sulky, arms swinging, belly out front.

"Aydin, there's a job for you. Friday at Zola's on Ku'damm, minding the door. Talk to Heiko." Before I answer he saunters away, slaps someone's back in passing and disappears.

Heiko is grinning at me from behind the bar, his blue eyes friendly but mocking in his pitted, orange sunbed face.

"You wanna do it?"

"What does it involve?" I ask.

"Involve? You just go to Zola's. You know Zola's?"

It's a big, famous nightclub I've never been to, so I just say yes because I wouldn't want him to know that I haven't ever been to a nightclub.

He continues: "Well, you go there on Friday. Stand at the door, look out for troublemakers and keep them out." He drafts a glass of something red then winks at me. "And let in all the beautiful girls. They'll thank you for it."

I laugh falsely and he laughs falsely. "What time?"

"Ten."

Two bodybuilders arrive and all three of them start to horse around and call raucously, which is embarrassing, seeing such big men behave like children. My heart's beating fast. I'm thinking what it might be like to be a professional bouncer. Then the Master reappears.

"Well?" He slaps my wet shoulder. He hardly needs to ask: I'm not about to say no.

He walks past, knowing my mind. Then he stops and turns back to me. "Listen," he adds, stepping up to me, taking my lapel between two fingers and looking at it closely, then raising his eyes to meet mine. "If there's any bother, forget hitting or kicking or any stuff like that. Get yourself a metal bar and if they really make trouble, you just hit them with the bar. But – " and he comes even closer, his face right in mine, " – not on the head. You hear? There'll be real trouble otherwise. Arms, legs," and he mimes swinging a bar and slaps his own upper arms and the sides of his knees, looking at me. "Hit their legs, break their legs. Then they'll be out of action. But not the head. You hear? We don't want any shit."

He doesn't wait for me to answer, he just laughs loudly, pats my wet shoulder, turns away and sways off down the corridor, his arms and ponytail swinging.

30

He's wearing rings on his thick fingers and chains on his wrists. Maybe now I'll be able to give up my rubbish press job and move to bigger things. That would show my parents, if I were to end up with money from a world they don't even know.

I'm only going to Café Abgang to talk to Slobodan, not to drink. I need to talk to him. He's not around. I sit at the bar inside and order a tea. Jürgen the barman is dour and busy drying up glasses in a rush. There's music playing and lots of smoke; people I don't know are playing chess and talking beneath the gloomy yellow lights. Then Slobodan comes out from the pool room at the back with a cigarette in hand, wearing his sleeveless leather jacket.

"What's that?" he says, pointing at the tea and slapping my arm. We shake hands and I laugh.

"Can't drink today, got to work early. How're you?"

He puts his unlit cigarette in his mouth and feels in his pockets, at the same time saying to the barman: "A beer for me, a korn for this pussy."

He lights his cigarette and looks affectionately at me. He's already had a few, I can tell by the redness in his eyes and his silly smile.

"Slobo, I've got a new job," I say.

"Oh yeah?" he grins. "What?"

"Bouncing at Zola's on Ku'damm."

"What? Wow. Bouncing at Zola's?" and he slaps my

arm again and sizes me up but seems unsure and suddenly a bit distant. "You're a fuckin' hardman, Aydin. You made it big."

I feel disappointed; I wanted him either to object, or celebrate, but not look doubtful.

"Should I do it?"

"Of course you should. Must be good money?"

"Dunno."

"What dya'mean dunno?" He blows out a great blast of smoke and frowns at me.

"The Master offered me the job. He didn't say how much."

Slobodan frowns even harder. "That's bullshit."

I'm annoyed at Slobodan now. I didn't want him to criticise. My korn arrives, climbing up the walls of its tiny glass. My stomach churns at the sight of it but I down it and swallow hard; fumes of alcohol kick back up my nose and make my eyes water. Slobodan looks surprised.

"Thought you weren't drinking?"

I put a five-mark coin on the bar and climb down.

"I'm not. Gotta go. See you."

He looks sad but says nothing. Then he calls after me.

"Aydin."

"Yes?"

"Watch yourself with Zola and those guys."

I'm walking home and I feel like talking to my father. Not about the job. About normal things. Leaving the bar early and not getting drunk makes me think of him. But when I get home he is not there.

2

So it's Friday night and I'm outside Zola's and this is what it's like: a long queue of ladylegs and guys in jostling denim, leather and T-shirts, hands in pockets, joking, showing off, pushing, dropping comments and being boisterous. At the door are two men twice my size who don't look like they need help. Maybe there's been a mistake; maybe the Master and Heiko were just playing a trick on me. I'm leaning on a lamp post some way off, rolling a smoke and watching them and watching the queue. They're letting people in by the batch, especially the girls, and they're stopping the occasional man to talk but I can't hear anything from this distance except the traffic swishing by on Kurfürstendamm and the swell of thumping music from inside the nightclub every time the door opens. There's the odd shout, cheer, whoop and laugh from the surging, growing queue.

My cigarette's nearly finished but I keep pulling on it until it burns my fingers then I toss it to the gutter. The last drag leaves an acrid bonfire taste. I still don't know what I'm going to say but I just walk over to the doormen. The furthest one's a Turk so I speak to him across the waiting guests.

"Evening."

The nearer bouncer holds out a flat palm towards my chest and looks at me. "The queue starts back there," and he flicks his head to gesture down the block.

Two skinheads next in line gawp at me.

"I've come to work," I say.

"What?"

The thumping is loud when the door opens. The skinheads stare. One has a tattoo of a battleaxe on the side of his head, a ring through the middle of his nose and some other tiny tattoos on his face; his arms are solid tattoo. I try not to look at him.

"I've come to work," I say.

I try to catch the eye of the Turkish bouncer but he's looking down the queue. The nearer bouncer has buzz-cut blond hair and is a good foot taller than me. His head is immense and he looks down at me, knotting the muscles of his eyebrows.

"Work? Who're you?"

"Aydin."

"Aydin? No Aydins work here. Get lost." He turns away.

"I'm from the gym in Neukölln."

He turns back to me. "What?" His voice is rising.

"The gym. Heiko. You know him?"

Then a skinhead spits some words at me: "Fuck off Aydin, you don't work here. Go back to fucking pleb Neukölln." The other bellows above the crowd: "And try going to the gym when it's fucking open, you skinny bastard!" There's some scattered laughter and the thumping goes on. The meaty-faced bouncer ushers them in, telling them to behave or go somewhere else, then turns back to the queue. Next in line are a number of bronzed legs. One of them winks at me and nudges her friend; she has a sparkly short blue dress on and blue eyes beneath a straight fringe of glossy, jet-black hair, and she has some kind of sparkly dust on her cheeks. They giggle and go in through the dark door into the thumping dungeon, smiling at me knowingly.

"I was sent by my karate teacher," I say. The bouncer turns quickly towards me and points at my chest. "Get lost!"

But the big silent Turk interrupts from across the queue. "Maybe he's the new boy." He's looking at me at last, sideways. His partner takes a step back and examines me from head to toe.

"Him? You're fuckin' kiddin me," he says.

The big Turk speaks up again: "What's the name of your karate teacher, brother?"

"Benjamin Lok."

Meat-face laughs. "Fuck me, it is." He looks me up and down again, then says to his Turkish friend: "Well, you can go and leave me with Mr Universe here. What's-your-name: stand where he's standing and keep your mouth shut. If there's trouble you just keep the queue moving while I deal with it."

The Turk nods to us and disappears into the thumping dungeon.

Meat-face and I stand there for what seems like an hour and he doesn't say a single word to me; he just lets people in and jokes with some of them, others he's business-like with. People don't seem to notice me, they just talk to him when they come next in line. I keep hoping there'll be some trouble so I can show him something, but there isn't. After a long time he looks at me.

"Wear black clothes tomorrow. You look like a punter."

After another hour there's no more queue, just the odd person appearing from out of the night. The thumping goes on from behind the door, its speed and intensity changing from time to time. I roll a cigarette.

"No smoking here," says meat-face, not looking at me. I tuck the rolled cigarette into my pouch. He glances at me. "You can take a break though and smoke inside the club or around the corner."

I walk off and light up my smoke. Cars go past along Kurfürstendamm. Where they're all driving to at midnight I don't know. This is an easy job. I could do more of this. After some time, a big, black, shiny car pulls up by the club and three men climb out simultaneously and march straight inside without even looking at meat-face. I flick away my stub and go back to him.

"Who were they?"

"One of them's the owner: your boss." He smiles.

"How much longer do we work for?"

"Until four or five."

"What's your name?"

"Andy."

I shake his massive hand. It's good to have a new friend.

The next hour drags on. With the door shut the thumping is more distant. Hardly anyone arrives. Then at around 1.30 the door bursts open and pukes out a gob of giddy girls, tumbling around and stroking our faces and shrieking and spilling off down the street, dancing. The door shuts again and the thumping goes distant. Half an hour later more people come out, then more and more. Then the skinhead pair burst out and tattoohead sees me and spits on my face and then saunters off. Then he turns around again and gives me the fist-sign.

"You don't get provoked, eh?" says Andy, examining me from out of the corner of his eye. I wipe my face, thinking of bacteria.

The next night we're standing there letting the queue in bit by bit when two young Turks around my age arrive from the side and try to get in but Andy stops them.

"Queue up like the others."

"Come on, let us in," whinges the one and tries again to enter. Andy stops him with a thick arm, which the Turk pushes. I try not to look.

"Let us in or I'll tell your boss, big chimpanzee," says the other Turk in a high, nasal voice. "I'm known here." I can't believe he's talking like that to such a massive man.

Andy takes a step forward so he's right up close to him and speaks at him right above his head. "Clear off."

The Turk shoves him but just propels himself backwards, then Andy moves forward startlingly fast and grabs the little Turk by the jacket; the other one runs up and kicks Andy in the arse but Andy ignores it. There are excited shouts of "Fight! Fight!" from the queue.

"Hey," I say to the second young Turk. Andy still has the first man by the jacket and they're facing each other. The second Turk glances at me: "What're you doin' here? Fuckin' traitor." I move towards him. Andy throws the other man off and they wait for a moment and look at us, then turn and leave, cursing us horribly.

The queue is all chatter, gossip and nervous laughter.

It's the following Friday at Zola's. The Master wasn't at training this week and work in the basement was boring. All week long I've been looking forward to tonight. We're standing here letting people in and the same two skinheads are in the queue and they get to us and the one who spat at me is staring at me, making his eyes go wide and twisting his head like a crazed owl. I look away and they go in.

At about two o'clock they come bursting out and the one with the tattooed head launches straight up to me and puts his face into mine so that his nose touches my nose and he shouts a noise into my mouth; some of his spit goes into my mouth and his breath smells like sick and cigarettes. Then he slaps me in the face and walks off. Some other people come out and stop to watch.

"Hey!" shouts Andy and goes after him but the other one shouts "Fascist!" and rushes at Andy. Andy turns towards him and tattoohead comes straight back and is trying to hit me now but I've got my guard up and I'm just absorbing blows with my hands and arms. "Fight, you fuckin' foreigner," he spits. "Fight." Then he shouts: "FUCK YOU!" I don't know how he can be so angry with someone he doesn't know. Andy's got the other one in a headlock now and that boy's thrashing like a cat in a trap. I look to Andy to see what to do but he's just holding the skinhead tight round the neck and looking down at the top of his shaven head.

"Shall I hit this one?" I shout.

"Yes," grunts Andy. The skinhead is thrashing and kicking him with his heels.

I shout at tattoohead: "Stop hitting me or I'll kill you," but he kicks me in the stomach and it really hurts and I double up and he knees me in the face and I back off and start shaking and I shout at the top of my voice at no one in particular, shake off the pain and clench my fists into rocks the way the Master teaches us. More people are watching us now, a whole crowd, and someone shouts that I should kill him; a girl shouts that he should kill me. I smell his sweat and odour and feel sick and angry, like I'm going to lose it – and I want to.

"Come on shit-arse Turk, hit me," says tattoohead.

I move in towards him and make a move to punch his face, which makes him flinch his hands up and I roar and kick his lower thigh the way Mario had tried to kick mine. He's not prepared for it at all, he just tries pathetically to sway his leg away from the blow. When my shin connects with the side of his knee, there's a loud snapping sound and his leg folds up sideways; some girls scream and spin away, covering their faces; some guys moan.

He's on the floor squirming, holding his knee and gasping for air, letting out short shrieks. His leg is all wrong. Its lower half flops limply outwards like a dead thing. The other skinhead has stopped struggling; his face is stone grey and his petrified eyes are glued to his writhing friend. I feel a bit nauseous. He looks so dirty and despicable writhing on the floor.

Later the police and an ambulance come and put him on a stretcher and take him away. The police invite me into their van which has a brown peeling Formica table and a stained coffee flask in it, as if they were out camping, and they ask me questions like what my name is, where I live and who I work for and I say I work for the club. They write lots of things down on forms and they sigh quite a bit and seem very tired – bored in fact. Andy pokes his head in through the driver's open window at the front and says I was defending myself but a policeman tells him quite sternly to go away. More people have gathered around the scene outside and are watching, hands in pockets, their peering faces coming and going in the flashing blue lights. The police tell me I've broken a man's leg and that I may have to come to court then they let me go and drive away, and I go back to the door of the club.

"Bruce fuckin' Lee," says Andy. "Should I hit him…? Should I hit him…? – then he breaks his leg! You're a bloody nut," he says, sinking his hands in his pockets and shivering. I pretend it's nothing. Later the boss comes out of the club and glances at me on his way to the waiting car. I wonder if he knows what I just did. He has dark, slicked-back hair and a very shiny navy suit which is cut perfectly to his body and he's with another man with short, white, receding hair and a deep tan who's wearing jeans and a new white shirt, open at the collar. There's another man with them who is tall and looks around above everyone's heads and into the middle distance, his eyes darting this way and that. He opens the door of the black car for the boss. I could do what he's doing, protecting the boss. After what I've just done, he'll want me around.

Later on, back home, as the first morning sunlight creeps into my room, I drop into a slanting sleep on my smelly pillow and dream that the skinhead has died and it's on the national news and I have to emigrate and never see my family again.

It's Tuesday afternoon and I've finished work at the department store; I arrive home and turn the key. I'm taking off my shoes in the carpeted corridor when my father comes out.

"Aydin," and he goes back into the lounge. I follow him with my head hanging.

"Father."

"What's all this with the police?"

He launches into talking without even sitting down, pacing around instead.

"They came round asking for you. And what's this black eye and this cut you've got? Come on boy, tell me."

He's looking at me, standing now in the middle of the room. I can hardly look at him.

"Come on, out with it."

"I got hit."

"And? What about the police? They said you injured someone."

"I did."

"How?"

"I kicked him."

"Kicked him and broke his leg, yes?" My father keeps staring at me. I can feel the fury he's holding. "This could get us in trouble Aydin. Where did this happen?"

"On Ku'damm."

"When?"

"Last Saturday night."

My father's voice rises further still. "What do you think you're doing on Kurfürstendamm on a Saturday night?"

"Working."

I shouldn't have told him, but I've got no defences with him.

"Working? That's no place for a Muslim to work. That's a place of ... That's a place of the devil," and his face begins to redden. I say nothing. He reverses unsteadily, lowers himself onto the sofa and looks up at the ceiling, his breathing laboured. "What have I done wrong that you always go to that? What have I done to deserve this?" he asks the ceiling.

I stay silent, frozen. He looks at me, his eyes verging on tears.

"You must not go out at night any more. You hear me?" and he gets up suddenly from the sofa but just stands there. He slaps his leg with his fist then leaves the room, then comes back in, shouting now. "You don't go out of this house now except to your real job, then you come straight back home. You hear? I won't have sinful behaviour under my roof." Then he leaves the room and slams the door but it's a thin door so it's more of a muffled bumping sound.

Later in bed I hear him and my mother talking urgently through the wall, their voices raised. My mother sobs and her voice goes up and down in a way I hate. I feel ashamed and sorry for my father and I wish I could talk to him but it's out of the question. They go on like that for a long time and I don't know whether I sleep at all that night.

The next day I skip training and come straight home from work and make a point of greeting my father and he returns the greeting coldly and doesn't smile. Then I watch TV with both of them to try to make amends, but they don't say a word and I feel suffocated. I hate the things they watch. On Thursday I come home and ask my father if I can please go to karate and he says yes but I must come straight back by eight thirty and eat a proper meal.

The Master is at the gym but he says nothing about Zola's or the skinheads or the boss. When I get home I eat silently with my parents and go to bed.

It's Friday at last. Today at the rubbish press I found a black square metal bar and took it home with me. It's nine in the evening now and I'm in my room. I slide the bar down inside my jeans and tighten my belt to trap it in place, but it hurts so I put it up the sleeve of my brown leather jacket then slip out of the apartment silently while my parents watch TV.

"What's that up your sleeve?" asks Andy when I arrive at Zola's.

"A metal bar," I say and let it slide out a little.

"And where are you going to put it when you take your jacket off?"

"Dunno. Thought it might be better to have it though."

"Not out here Aydin. The guys inside carry bars but not ones like that."

I prop the bar behind a drainpipe some way away and we do our shift. Late in the night some drunks spill out of the thumping cavern and one of them shouts abuse at me and makes to push me but his friend holds him back and says to him "watch it, he's that psycho," and pulls him away saying "snapped someone's knee, brother. Bone came out." His friend goes limp and walks away, looking back over his shoulder.

Some time after that the boss emerges and smiles at me and pats my arm as he walks past, but says nothing. He must know what I did. I've not even been into Zola's yet – but tomorrow night is Saturday and I'm going to.

Saturday night. The bronze legs with the short blue silvery dress and jet black hair just went into the club and smiled and said Hi to me on the way. Her legs and blue eyes make me want to just follow her straight in. Her friends are background noise. But the real reason I want to follow her is because she remembered me.

At break time I tell Andy I'm going into the club to smoke and he grins and opens the door for me.

I step into a dark, down-sloping tunnel with black-painted plywood walls, walking against a blast of sound and a wind of hot underground air full of smoke and beer mingled with things I have never smelled before. As the door swings shut behind me it makes a counter-wind and my eardrums are thumped – thumped – thumped. Up ahead lasers and green flashing lights stagger on-off-on-off through vapour clouds. The tunnel opens out into a black cavern surrounded by a gallery where I now stand, looking dizzily down into a pit of writhing and thrashing bodies. I am buried in sound; there is no space to speak or even think; the thumping consumes all and everything, above a changing tonal growl beneath. I look down at the pit of slamming bodies seeking the blue silvery dress who noticed me. There are hundreds of human specimens there, all moving frantically. Around the edges of the pit people are making their way somewhere holding drinks and cigarettes. I can't see her.

To my right are stairs leading down into the pit and I descend. The sound is at its peak here. All the

walls are matt black, the heat and moisture stifling. I'm
pushing between agitating bodies who laugh and shout
and throw back their heads and wave their arms and
swirl their hips and jump on the spot and point in the
air and shuffle their hands and give intimate looks to
the beat of the thumping. I light a cigarette to occupy
my mouth and begin to walk around the perimeter,
right, right around. She is not anywhere. At one end
of the pit is a bar three-deep with cramming bodies, at
the other is a stage with a DJ and his equipment and,
surveying the pit, two men dressed in black like me;
they each nod as I pass them by.

Leading off the long sides of the thumping pit are
four exits with signs above them. I enter the one called
The Garage. Down a passage is a different, smaller
cavern containing a screeching hissing sound with
pumping and howling vocals, where a different set of
bodies are thrashing harder and shaking their long hair
in a strobe light and it smells of sweat, fear and aggres-
sion. I don't think she will be in here.

The second entrance is called The Teapot and leads
to a dark roomful of lava lamps and sofas and bean-
bags draped with slinking bodies smoking and laughing and the music is all jelly and swell. I wend my way
through clouds of sweet-smelling grassy smoke, past
faces that look through me but hers is not one of them.

Back to the thumping pit. The third entrance is The
Control Room and leads to a calmer, roomier place
with alcove seating within giant cut-out beer vats the

size of garden sheds; this room has its own bar behind which a young man stoops, shaking something. There are hardly any people here but in one vat I catch sight of the slick-haired owner engrossed in conversation with someone I don't know. There are two women with them – but not her.

The fourth passage leads to The Chill, where the sound is underwater cool white and many girls and a few boys chat on easy seating and there she is, the girl who noticed me, her bronze gazelle's back facing me, sitting with three friends around a neon coffee table, laughing and drinking. The girl sitting opposite her sees me as I enter and leans in, says something and laughs and the four of them all look around. But the girl who noticed me turns away again and continues to chat, pointing far to the side with her cigarette and tapping ash on the floor. The opening down the middle of her dress goes right down to the channel of the small of her back. I wonder what it's like there.

My heart is in my mouth. I look at her tanned nape where her short black bob finishes but I don't know how to approach it and I'm afraid she might have already forgotten me and her friends might mock me, and I'm running out of time before her friends start thinking I'm a creep for looking, so I turn away and go back to the thumping pit. One of the two bouncers is no longer on the stage. Up the stairs I go, onto the gallery and back along the dark, uphill corridor. The door at the end opens to reveal a bulky silhouette which speaks to me as I pass.

"Andy's waiting."

I gasp the fresh air outside on the street.

"Where were you? I'm dying for a piss," says Andy and disappears into the club. The queue is still there, all their eyes on me. I don't know why I couldn't just talk to her.

Monday evening and the Master comes into the dojo. We're all lined up. Without a word of welcome it's "Fifty press-ups – inner two knuckles on wood." All nine of us move to the edge of the mat and put our knuckles down on the wooden strip. By thirty-five someone's struggling and moaning, by forty most are, and by forty-five, people are slumping down.

"Continue!" roars the Master and there is a loud slap and a grunt of surprise from someone. "Eyes ahead." I stare at the skirting board for forty-seven, forty-eight, forty-nine, fifty, then jump up flexing my fingers and rubbing my knuckles. We move back to our places, panting, some hanging heads, some suppressing moans. The Master paces quickly back and forth at the front, his eyes darting, bamboo sword in hand, then he turns to Lars and without warning hits him viciously on the arm, rapping the bamboo canes.

"Guard up!" he shouts. Lars complies without a sound and everyone else does the same.

"Now squat, come up, front kick, squat, come up,

front kick. Eighty. Go! – Iche, nee, san, shi, go, rocku."

Up and down we bob, kicking each time at the space in front.

The Master shouts again: "Harder!" and he lifts his shinai to threaten someone.

"Stop, stop," he says. "Stop." He comes to the front, sighing, and turns to face us, folding his arms.

"What's that supposed to be?"

Then he squats sloppily, lazily, ogling at the ceiling, then comes up and flops his foot out in front.

"What's that? Eh?" He glares around our faces. "What kind of a kick is that?" He faces me. "Aydin, tense your stomach – " I brace myself with one leg back; the kick sends me crashing into the man behind who falls over onto the mat but I remain upright, my guard up, proud.

"Again – with ki-ai. Iche, nee, san, shi."

With each kick we scream the war cry.

Forty minutes later and I'm struggling to stand for exhaustion. There are pools of sweat all over the room.

"Okay good," says the Master, smiling. "Very good. That's how you have to be. For some of you there's a tournament in two weeks' time. Full-contact, three-minute bouts, no headgear. There'll be prize money. Whoever trains well this week will get selected. Have a good evening."

The next day I'm all aches and bruises but I force

myself to train, the same on Wednesday. On Thursday he talks to us before the class, telling us it's all in the head: if you're fighting and you get hurt or injured you just have to put it away and keep going. Then we spar ferociously in pairs and I knock somebody onto the mat with a punch to the side of his head. He goes off and holds his head in his hands and I feel peculiar and a bit sorry.

On Friday I have a fever. My whole body is wracked with shuddering aches and my head throbs. I come home early from the department store, skip training and call Andy to excuse myself from Zola's. Then I sleep until midday the next day.

When I wake up I go straight out to avoid my parents but I've nothing to do and I feel isolated and afraid, so I call Slobodan from a payphone. The sky is grey and orange and steamy and thunder is grumbling. He says meet him at Hasenheide for breakfast. I say it's the afternoon and he says so what.

Slobodan's eyes are even more bloodshot than usual, the rims of his eyelids are red and he reeks of cigarettes and beer. His cropped hair seems thinner and his scalp greasy.

"Where were you last night?" he asks.

"I was sleeping. I was ill."

"And last weekend and all week long? You abandoned Slobo?"

"I was working at Zola's last weekend and training all week for a tournament."

He looks surprised and annoyed. "You took the job at Zola's? How is it?"

"It's… it's good I suppose. I'm going again tonight."

"You look worn out. Worse than me."

I say nothing, just look away. Our food and beers arrive. It's hard to talk to him in the daylight and he looks dishevelled and depressed but I don't feel I can ask why. With Slobo, it's as if there's something beneath the surface which you wouldn't want to see, which he keeps carefully hidden away. Whatever it is, it's about the only thing he's tidy and careful about. The rest of him is neglectfully strewn about. Afterwards he buys a frisbee from an African street seller outside the underground and we go into the park and throw it back and forth to each other, further and further, until a dog comes rushing across and jumps high in the air and catches it, then trots off chewing it. The dog's punk owner gives us the finger as he stalks by. I start heading towards him to challenge him, but Slobodan jogs over to intercept me.

"Leave it Aydin."

The punk has stopped and is staring at us. His dog is one of those fighting breeds.

"Can't he control his bloody dog?" I protest. Slobodan holds my arm firmly.

Then a group of four other punks saunter over, materialising as if from nowhere, a collection of black, torn, skinny jeans, tattoos, chains, studs and dyed, spiky hair.

"What's your fuckin' problem?" demands one as they half encircle us.

Slobodan still has hold of my arm. Now there are five of them, I'm scared, but Slobodan holds me firm.

"No problem," he says. "No problem. You got a problem?" His hold on my arm feels less like a restraint now and more like reassurance.

"You not like my dog?" asks the first punk.

"Of course I like your dog," says Slobodan. "Staffie. I've got a bulldog. Love 'em," and he smiles and stuffs his hand in his pocket and pulls out his tobacco, releases my arm and starts pulling a tuft of shag from the packet and rolling a cigarette, taking his time, relaxed. The punks watch. "Want one?" says Slobodan, offering the packet to the punk nearest to him. The pallid young man steps forward and takes it. Slobodan lights his cigarette, stuffs his hands in his pockets and puffs some smoke out of the side of his mouth, just standing there, smiling. He's a head taller than any of them. They start to lose interest and saunter off, the dog panting happily behind. I want to go after them to retrieve the tobacco but he holds my arm again and smiles.

"Leave it. They're just boys."

People are walking all over the park. Thunderclouds are mounting in the warm sky above. We walk on for a while but there's not much to do now our frisbee is gone. I don't really know how to say goodbye to Slobodan so I say I have to go to work and he shrugs and looks away and I watch him wander off and I miss him already, but I just don't know how to be with him without drinking. Does he even have any other friends? What a waste of a good man. There's so much of him I don't know about. How can he be so calm with hostile people like that?

The first big drops of warm rain are falling, hissing one by one into the dizzy grass. People in the park begin to up and move, folding away rugs hurriedly and doing up bra straps. One old man on a bicycle wobbles along briskly, holding a newspaper over his head.

I walk without purpose, submitted to the rain, and come to the gates of a rambling cemetery. An old lady shuffles in before me with a bouquet of flowers, oblivious to the downpour which makes her flowers nod. I follow her slowly. She shuffles on up the pathway between the markers of bones.

The bones must mostly belong to Berliners from before the city was cut in half. Now they're buried in the West and the Wall has just come back down. Easterners are flooding into the West like water, filling every hole, but the bones don't care.

A pungent scent rises off the warm tar path in the summer rain and carries me blissfully away.

Zola's, Saturday night. It's still raining and the streets
are wet and hot. Andy is letting people in fast, hardly
questioning anyone. The blue dress who noticed me
doesn't come; I regret being a coward last week and
not talking to her. We get rained and rained on and
slowly grow cold despite the warmth. Endless traffic
splashes past along Kurfürstendamm. At break time
I go straight inside to get warm, down the thumping
tunnel, down the steps and into the hot pit. I wonder
what it's like here in the day when it's quiet and empty,
with its black plywood walls and beer-stained floor? I
shiver; water has seeped right through to my under-
wear.

I go into The Control Room where it's quieter and
empty and I sit at the bar. The thumping comes in
down the entrance tunnel. A barman offers me a drink
but the sight of the bottled spirits ranked behind him
makes me feel like vomiting, so I just ask for a coke.

The dark red carpet is sticky and the beer vats,
which from here I cannot see into, look like they're
wet with something like creosote. I begin to wonder
who might be in them – and whether I might sit in one
and enjoy its cushioned privacy, so I get up and walk
along the right-hand row. They're all occupied by chatting groups. I go around the far end and come back
along the other row. The first vat has just one man in
it, staring fixedly at a glass. The second is empty so I
go inside and sit on the red velvet upholstery. It's even
more muffled in here, the thumping is far away but I

feel wrong sitting alone so I come out. As I approach the last vat I stop in my tracks: the girl who noticed me is sitting there with her bronze, muscular legs crossed, her blue hem half-way up her leg and someone's hand on it. She's smoking and laughing. She sees me and looks at me for a second, then turns back to nodding at what someone is saying. I move further to see the slick-haired, suited boss with his hand on her thigh. He checks me for a second. Sitting next to him, central in the vat, his feet planted squarely, legs wide apart, is the Master, wearing a different midnight-blue shirt and the same thick gold chains on his chest as the other day, heavily ringed hands placed flat on the table in front of him. He stares at me impassively for a moment, his face completely flat, and my stomach seizes up, the hairs on my back stand on end. Then his face breaks into a smile and he laughs loudly.

"Aydin Mesüt. Aydin Mesüt! Come here, Aydin Mesüt. Sit down with us, meet Zola," and he claps a big hand on the club owner's razor-sharp shoulder. "Meet the lovely Steffi," and he gestures to the girl. Her eyes sparkle at me and she mouths a silent "hello". Zola shifts his hand on her leg and looks stern. To the Master's right is a young, pale, thin, blonde woman looking tired and apologetic and wearing scant clothing that reveals most of the details of a malnourished figure.

"Na Zola? Told you I had the best boys for you," says the Master. "Sit!" His voice is too loud. I perch myself on a stool at the corner opposite Steffi and say nothing.

"Aydin's in shock," says the Master to the others, "because he only knows me from the dojo. Doesn't know this is my place too. No Aydin?"

"Yes," I say, paralysed.

"A man of few words is our Aydin Mesüt," he continues, "but a big heart. Have a drink Aydin." Then he stands up and shouts very loudly, "Pattie!" and sits back down.

"No thanks, I just had one."

"What?" says the Master, then stands up again and roars out – "PATTIE!"

A woman arrives in a hurry. "Yes Benny?"

"A drink for Aydin here. What do you want?" and he gives me a disapproving look, so I ask for a beer and the woman goes away.

"Aydin here's a fighter, no Aydin? There'll be no trouble while he's on your door, eh? In fact," he says, looking at Zola, an excited smile breaking his face, "he's the answer to what you were talking about. You want more work Aydin? Eh?" Then he laughs.

I do want more work. That's what I want. But something pins me to my seat, mute.

"Come on Aydin," he continues, "don't be gloomy, Zola's got work for you, you want work don't you? What's your day job?"

"I work at a department store in Neukölln."

"A department store in Neukölln? A department

store in Neukölln?" He appears to be trying to remember something. "What, let me guess… downstairs, yes? I know, let me guess – down in the basement on the forklift, yes?"

"The cardboard press." I omit the rubbish press.

"The cardboard press! The cardboard press! And what do they pay you to work on the cardboard press, Aydin Mesüt? Huh? Nine marks an hour? Ten? Good money eh?" and he turns to his colleague and laughs a hollow, false laugh. Steffi crosses her legs towards me and looks concerned, but Zola still has his hand on her thigh and he stares at me unflinchingly, examining me coldly.

"Aydin. Zola here will give you five hundred deutschmarks just to go and pick up some money, no Zola?"

Still watching me, Zola speaks with an Eastern Bloc accent I can't place: "Okay. Let's try 'im."

"You alright with that Aydin?" says the Master, shifting forward and scrutinising my face. Then he speaks even more loudly: "You alright with that?"

"I dunno," I say, my veins filling with fear and hope. "What do I have to do?"

I glance at Steffi. Her eyes are imploring me to do something, but I don't know what.

"It's simple," says the Master, leaning back again, taking a pen from the table and scrawling on a beer mat. "You go Monday morning to this address in Charlottenburg, nice and early mind, nine o'clock or so, and you say you've come for Zola's money."

He grins. I feel sick. I don't want to go.

"It's no use Benny," says Zola blankly, still staring at me, "he's not going to do it. He doesn't know what to do," and he looks away across the room, bored.

The Master sighs, puts his hands back on the table and leans back.

"Okay, I'll do it, but Aydin's coming with me so he can learn how to do your shit jobs next time." The Master looks at me. "Meet me at Kaiserdamm underground station on Monday at nine."

"Alright," I reply automatically. The two men stare at me and I realise they want me to leave. The waitress arrives with my beer and looks confused as I rise and walk away. Steffi gives me a sad smile goodbye. Now I want to talk with her even more.

3

Late Sunday morning. I'm trying to get back to sleep.
I turn my pillow over for the cooler side then put my
head under it, but then I can't breathe. There's a knock
on my door and in comes my father. He sits on the end
of my bed.

"Uncle Mejid's coming for lunch in an hour. Will
you be here?"

I sit up and run my hand through my hair. "Yes.
Yes, I'll be here."

"Good," he says, and pats my leg then leaves.

My pillow cover has been washed and no longer
smells. Mother still takes care of me, whatever I do.
Uncle Mejid: he's worth staying in for. I hide in my
room until I hear the visitors arrive.

My mother brings dish after dish from the kitchen onto the dining room table: beans in a pale red sauce, köfte still sizzling from the pan, stuffed vine leaves, rice in steaming mounds, bulgur wheat, eggs, lamb stew fragrant with rosemary, cucumber salad and olives from a cousin's shop, swimming in oily brine, and from somewhere the smell of fried garlic wafts in. My mouth waters. Uncle Mejid is wearing a round knitted white skullcap that grips the top of his head. He does look similar to father but his hair hasn't turned grey and sometimes he lets his beard grow a little; today there's just prickly stubble. Father is always clean-shaven except his grey moustache.

Uncle's wife Selma has remained beautiful despite middle age and motherhood. She has emerald eyes and skin the colour of a Siamese cat and her headscarf is always colourful; today it's a turban patterned with green peacocks intertwisted with golden and olive-coloured vines. My mother was once beautiful too: you can see by the faded black and white wedding photos. But she hasn't stayed young like Aunt Selma.

Table talk is all about my cousins: who's had babies, where they've been on holiday, two cousins at university and my brother Ahmet – who thankfully isn't here. I probably love him, but I can't stand him. He's successful. Hard-working. Popular. He always knows where he's going and why, and he gets a lot of money and a lot of approval.

"He's found his feet in business," says my father.

"He's more ambitious than I was. He's tendered for removing sections of the old Wall between here and Rudow."

I already know where this conversation is going to end up.

"Really?" My uncle raises his big black eyebrows. "Didn't think you did government jobs?"

"I always thought they weren't our thing," says my father, "but he's got different ideas and I'm not going to stand in his way."

Mother makes an approving face and nods, eating morsels. I can sense her lining up the words about all the things I'm not achieving. She does it indirectly so I can't react.

"In fact," says father, finishing a mouthful, "he and his friend are doing a proposal for a housing development in some of the space where the border strip was."

"Hope they check for landmines," says my uncle, glancing at me and smiling, and they all laugh. He's joking, but he's trying to steer things in another direction. He also knows where they're heading.

"Ahmet's just doing so well," continues father. "He's already turning over more money than me. And did you see the revamp he did on Kochstrasse? It's been noticed by people in high places."

"So Aydin," purrs Aunt Selma. "You're not going to join them in the business?"

Here we go. There is the sound of cutlery on plates and chewing.

My uncle smiles. "No," he says, "Aydin's his own man," and he winks at me.

"A bit too much his own man I think," says father to his plate.

"No, no," replies Uncle Mejid warmly with a chuckle. "Don't you worry about him – hey Aydin?"

"Hmm," I say, eating without hunger.

"Well," says mother, looking at everyone except me with that indignant, resigned expression of hers. "Ahmet will make us proud."

She just can't help herself. And I can't help hitting back.

"Meaning," I say, looking at Uncle Mejid, "I won't."

"Aydin!" says father testily.

"Well," I reply, putting down my knife and fork. "You've never been proud of me. Why pretend? And you always compare me with Ahmet."

Father looks furious and guilty, so I add: "Did your parents compare you and Uncle Mejid like this?"

"Don't you dare say that!" squawks mother.

Everyone's stopped eating. My uncle holds out his palms and pats down the air.

"It's okay," he says. "Let's change the subject."

"Yes," I say, "let's change the subject, since talking about your parents is banned. I'm the only Turk in the world who doesn't know their grandparents."

My father gets up, hurls his napkin onto his chair and storms out of the room.

"Now look what you've done," says mother, getting

up and following him out.

Uncle Mejid and Aunt Selma have resumed eating again, in silence. I eat a mouthful more but my stomach doesn't want it.

"Sorry," I say eventually, pushing my chair back. Uncle Mejid looks sadly at his plate. I glance at him and think of tomorrow's date with Benjamin Lok at Kaiserdamm and I think of the cardboard press at the department store standing idle, how the trolleys will mount up, my boss angrily on the phone. I wish I could tell Uncle Mejid about Benjamin Lok, but he's always with other people.

I'm back in my bedroom and there's a knock at my door, but it doesn't open.

"Come in."

"It's me," says my uncle's voice.

"Come in."

He closes the door softly behind him and sits where my father sat.

"I said to them I'd have a word with you. They're worried about you. The late nights, the fighting; you know, the usual things. I told them not to worry but they do."

He waits for me to say something then continues, shrugging. "Anyway, here I am. If you need anything you let me know, yes?"

It's not even the grandparent taboo that bothers

me. All that talk of Ahmet does; it drives me mad; but just now I've got other worries. In my mind I see the Master sitting in the beer vat and I nearly say something to my uncle about him and the debt collecting, but I pull it back from the tip of my tongue.

"Just remember," he adds, "they love you even if it doesn't seem like it."

There are many things I'd like to say to Uncle Mejid, but my mouth is stuck. Most of the time he seems so cheerful. He has some hidden spark. He's like my father but without a cloud hanging over him. I'd like to be more like him and I'd like to have a beautiful wife like him.

"And," he continues, "they're worried about your faith."

"I do have faith," I reply without thinking. It's probably a lie, but it might not be.

"I know, Aydin, I know you do." He smiles and shrugs. "I said I'd talk to you and here I am."

"I just don't want to do things the way they do," I say.

"What does that mean?" he asks.

"It's just, it's just… Imam Osman – the mosque, the way everything's so… I dunno."

Uncle Mejid watches me.

"I dunno," I continue. "I just don't want to do things the way they do. And then they always criticise me…"

"I understand," says my uncle, patting my leg like

father. He sits for a while in silence, looking at me thoughtfully. Uncle Mejid's silence is reassuring.

"I promised your parents," he says, leaning in a little and lowering his voice, "a long time ago, never to talk with you about your grandparents." He hesitates. "But I'll tell you one thing. They were fighters like you. That's why your mother and father worry about you getting into trouble – because they don't want to lose you."

Then he stands up and looks at me. "You go on being who you are, Aydin," he says, looking at me with the faintest hint of a smile. "You'll find your own way." He leaves, closing the door carefully.

Uncle Mejid always makes things better. After he and my aunt have left the apartment I wonder for a long time about my grandparents and who they could have been, then I go to the bathroom and, as an experiment, start washing myself for the prayer, not for Uncle Mejid and definitely not for my parents; just to see what it's like to do it for myself. I make sure I don't make any sound they might hear. It's amazing how you don't forget things from childhood. But when it comes to taking off my socks to wash my feet, I lose heart and it seems pointless and I give up and go back to my room. I try to sleep but I just toss and turn, then I get up and go out onto the street.

I bump into some old acquaintances from school and go to the park and play football with them. I come back tired, sweaty and happier, but soon evening arrives and I start thinking about tomorrow and debt collecting with the Master.

There's nothing on TV. My room seems stuffy and small and I don't know what to do as the seconds mount up and pile up into minutes and hours. I set my alarm for 6.00 a.m. and decide to think about debt collecting in the morning. But sleep is slow in coming.

I'm running down Kurfürstendamm in the driving rain ahead of a front line of traffic which beeps, its tyres rasping and spitting road-film engines rumbling in the night closing in but I can't get off the road, I can't get off the road because there are walls or barriers so why can't I go to the pavement... they're closing on me and I've tattooed my face and arms. As I run I gape at my hands all drizzling with ink and rain and the road's sloping down where it shouldn't slope down towards the Memorial Church and the Mercedes Star turning atop the tower block, tourists churning on the square, bands busking and squatters smoking in dark doorways. If I could only get back home to my folks and their warmth; now I'm crying, they've locked the apartment door, they've left me out on the landing crying tears upon tears, curled up in a ball among the shoes.

I awaken on a wet pillow. My alarm is calling out 6.00 a.m., I jolt up and stumble to the bathroom; no time for any prayer washing now; clothes on, no stomach for food so I go, I leave for work and when I get there at ten to seven I loiter in a concealed spot near the entrance; it's eight minutes to clock-in time. Benjamin Lok is maybe rising with his woman wherever he lives, ready to make his way to meet me at nine in a different part of town. Downstairs the clock is ticking and the cards must be stamping and chinging six minutes to seven, Monday morning, start of the grind. People I recognise shuffle in through the workers' roll-up door: there's the canteen lady, and the Master said five hundred deutschmarks — if not for this job then for the next job and that's a whole week's work in the bowels of the department store; in goes the foreman who works behind the glass and never smiles at me. My heart is in a vice, my throat is hurting, the workers to whom I belong don't know about my abandoning them and I'm frightened. If I go in here now, the Master's eyes will say I'm a loser; if I go in here now, I face the Same, the Same, the Same; the creased Croatian cleaning lady who smiles and says the same wrong German things over and over every morning, she looks at me as she hurries in and it's two-minutes-to.

Then I remember Steffi, the blue dress bronze-legged girl at Zola's who liked me, who looked at me, concerned for me. I turn my back on the department store and walk away.

I meet the Master at Kaiserdamm tube station. He tells me sternly to call him Benny which I don't like, but I say okay. We jog up the steps and emerge onto a wide street roaring with traffic. He says just watch and learn. We go down some side streets. Coming here with him feels even more surreal than last night's dream. The tenements here look more affluent than Neukölln's: there's scrolling and engraving on the stone and the windows are larger and older but well painted; many of them have potted greenery dripping down from the sills. Maybe they dropped fewer bombs in this district, to spare the richer people, so there was less to rebuild. In the apartments I see bookcases and paintings and high ceilings and in one room a ceiling rose and a chandelier, in another a great black angular lamp taller than a man, in another a rubber plant. This is not a place where Turks live. Who can all these people be who live tucked away in luxury like this? The shops here sell expensive things that I cannot understand people buying, like a long, camel-coloured coat for two thousand deutschmarks, and angular, stainless steel coffee tables sitting in shop windows, on sale for one and a half thousand marks. The people walking around here are all dressed in expensive clothes and they are in a hurry, so they don't seem to notice the expensive things in the windows.

We enter an archway and go straight up some wide marble steps with teak banisters, passing a suited man on the way down who doesn't look at us, his heels clack-

ing the steps – certain of where he's going like successful people are. Or maybe he's escaping from us. On
the first floor there's a heavy, ornate wooden door with
a polished brass knob and knocker which the Master
raps sharply. I see some tiny pink wellington boots and
a little pair of girls' sandals lined up neatly on the landing alongside a lady's shoes and a pram, filling me with
dread. At the spyhole I see a change of light and there's
a sound then the door opens a few inches on a chain
and out peeps a woman's eye and a slice of face.

"Good morning Birgit," says the Master smoothly.
"Open the door please."

"What do you want?" she says in a sleepy quavering
voice.

"Are your parents in?"

"No. Can you go away?"

"Open the door Birgit, we need to chat."

"No… What do you want?"

Next to the tiny footwear on the landing is a little plastic elephant looking balefully up at us as if he
knows what's coming. The Master takes some steps
back then marches up to the door and his foot moves
so fast I don't realise what's happening and there's a
bang and a scream and the door is wide open with the
woman sprawled on the floor of the flat in her dress-
ing gown. There's a high-pitched, urgent voice from
a room somewhere in the back: "Mummy, mummy!"
The Master stands over the female heap and bawls at it.

"Give me Zola's five thousand."

She whimpers, covering her face with her hands and convulsing away from the Master.

"Mummy!" cries a little girl's voice from somewhere further inside the flat, but the child does not appear.

"Get me the money you useless bitch."

The woman drags herself up and staggers away, the Master following her, his long pigtail dangling down the back of his black leather jacket, moving towards where the child's voice is. I think about trying to do something to him, but I feel paralysed. Instead I just follow like in a dream. We enter a bedroom where the woman is already rummaging in a cupboard. There is a little hump beneath the bedspread, which moves and then goes silent except for the faintest of stifled little girl sobs. The Master sees the hump and goes towards it and I'm about to jump on him and attack him come what may, but he just pats it and says, "Don't worry, mummy's being a good girl." Then Birgit hands him a small wad of notes, her face smeared with tears, old mascara and blood. She looks past him at the bed-spread hump with terrified eyes.

"That's better," says the Master, changing his tone completely. "Why didn't you give it to him in the first place?"

"I needed it for someone else," whimpers Birgit, clutching a white, glossy windowsill for support. I can see her legs trying not to give.

The Master approaches her and she flinches and screws her eyes shut as he embraces her. "Don't cry, it's all over now, you come back to Zola, he says he misses you."

She weeps silently but says nothing and we leave. The hump in the bedclothes is still and almost silent – just the faintest sniffle.

"Cheer up, Aydin," says the Master, clapping me on the back once we're out in the street. "You shouldn't feel sorry for people, she's not the angel you think. She dances at Zola's other place. She looks different wrapped around a pole. I'll take you there, it's hot, you'll like it," and he chuckles, his eyes simmering. "Women – they're all trash." The air outside seems cold and strange smelling, the people hurrying about their normal business are like affluent aliens, the whole grey city like another planet. I want to protest about the little child but my mouth is clamped shut.

Instead I say: "Where are we going?"

"You can go home and sleep, what do you think? Have a lie-in. Here," and he pulls out the money and peels off two hundred mark notes and gives them to me. I'm on autopilot and can't decline; and it's two days' wages at the department store. I make up my mind to go straight back there and beg for my job.

"Thank you," I say, turning down the steps into the echoing, bleach-smelling U-Bahn station.

"Better than crushing rubbish all day," calls the Master, his voice rebounding off the tiled pissy walls.

In the darkness of the basement at the department store my former boss is clearing trolleys with his own bare hands. He refuses to talk to me or even look at me and says never, ever come back. Then, when I'm turning to go, he says there are East Berliners who want to work and that I should go back to Turkey now that they're coming.

I wander the streets and spend some money on breakfast but my stomach feels so tight I can't eat more than a few mouthfuls, so I sit on a doorstep in the sunshine and toss flat-bread morsel by morsel to a growing assembly of pigeons. At least I can be kind to them. I'll have to wait until five before going home, otherwise there'll be questions, so I just walk and walk and end up at Hermannplatz then head up into Kreuzberg. There are so many Turkish shops here. Mostly they look tired and shabby. I stop at one to buy a banana and sit on another doorstep to eat it. A group of Turkish men come out of a doorway and go their separate ways, some removing and pocketing skullcaps; it's just gone midday prayer, there must be some kind of mosque in that building. An old German couple go slowly by, oblivious.

Further along the street is a tucked-away art-house cinema I've often seen so I enter without thinking and watch a black and white Japanese film set in the world of business and family life full of dojo courtesy. There are only two other people in the cinema. The film is slow-moving but touching and I feel settled when I come out into the orange daylight.

At training that evening the Master is not there, which is disappointing. I train extra hard, doing everything to the limit. I hit and kick my partner as hard as I can and he hits me back but eventually he can't take it and complains about me. The substitute teacher takes me as his own partner and kicks me in the stomach and I kick him back and I can tell he's struggling not to lose his temper. Then he gives the class a long, boring lecture.

I leave feeling sick at the prospect of days without work and trying to rid my head of the bump beneath the bedclothes and the little girl's sobs. The following days I spend roaming the snide streets of Neukölln and Kreuzberg, fruitlessly asking for work and trying to avoid Turkish people who might know me.

On one of the days I go through the backstreets to look at the Wall. There's a wooden viewing tower next to it, so I climb up. Its little covered platform is just at the level of the top of the Wall, so you can gaze out over the strip that lies beyond, which is as wide as a football pitch and the colour of sand. Coils of barbed wire meander along it, and some rusting iron Czech hedgehogs lie strewn randomly, apparently to stop tanks that might want to come, but I wouldn't know where they would come from. Then there are the watchtowers, much higher than this one, where soldiers used to wait, their rifles shouldered. Beyond these are large buildings reaching away into the maze of streets, thousands of windows, all full of people who have grown up in the East, a different country – a different continent. There is a service road along the far side of the strip, and along it walk two soldiers, one with an Alsatian on a lead, still pointlessly following the old routine.

On Thursday I bump into Imam Osman in a news-agent and he greets me coldly and asks whether my parents know I'm not at work. Later at home the air's like an electric storm and my mother greets me with a look I can't bear. Just as I'm about to go to sleep at night, my father enters my room without knocking and tells me that if I'm not going to work then I have to go to the mosque with him tomorrow.

It's Friday and I'm entering the mosque for the first time in months, maybe even a year. It's an industrial building hidden away behind some tenements. I'm be-ing carried slowly along in a dense flow of men. The smell of scent mingles with the smell of shoes at the entrance, then as we get further into the mosque a calmness descends. The carpet is expansive and I sit on the far side and fall to contemplating the week gone by. Then Imam Osman comes in and takes his place at a lectern in a raised niche at the front, from which he peers down over the growing congregation like a judge in a courtroom, his reading glasses perched on the end of his nose, his plastic turban shining beneath the buzzing fluorescent lights.

He taps the microphone. "Brothers and sisters!" he begins in a potent voice completely different from his usual one. Then after the customary salutations in Arabic he continues in Turkish: "The worst sin is to be idle. The good Muslim works hard to earn his keep and feed his family and keeps away from the evils and temptations of Satan and," then he raises the pitch of his voice a bit, "he keeps his eyes off naked flesh and keeps away from fornication. Hellfire awaits those who fall into the ways of the degenerates who disobey their parents. We lack faith and we spend too much time following the ways of the disobedient."

I look around for my father but cannot see him. The faces of the congregation look apprehensively up at the Imam or down at their socks. Some wiggle their toes, some pick at the carpet. Imam Osman's words go on and his pitch rises by a few degrees every minute until after a while he's hurling a crescendo of warnings. I begin to daydream of mountains, then I think of Steffi, then of the fighting tournament next week and I wonder what it will be like trying to knock out someone I don't know. Then I find my eyelids heavy like stones and my head nodding in the heat and airlessness of amassed bodies. At last the call to prayer comes, piercing the thick air and everyone stands and we pray and Imam Osman's voice comes over the speakers as he recites verses in yet another voice, and we bow and prostrate. With my head on the carpet I feel safe from him and everyone.

After the prayer I run into some former friends and we eat together in the canteen and laugh and I forget everything.

That night I get to Zola's before Andy and wait. People come in dribs and drabs at first, then a queue slowly forms and Andy arrives. He seems tired. After an hour Steffi arrives alone wearing a different, thinner dress through which I can see more of her shape but she doesn't queue, she just comes from the side and Andy lets her straight in. She smiles at me but looks distracted, then disappears into the thumping dungeon, from which clouds of vapour are billowing.

At break time I go straight in, determined to find her and talk to her. She's dancing with girlfriends on the dance floor so I brace myself and join them, and immediately she puts her arms around my neck and I feel her hips touching mine.

"Hi," she shouts, her face inches from mine.

"Hi," I shout back.

"Come looking for me?"

"Yes."

She flicks her hair back and smiles. She's chewing gum and has strong shoulders. I can smell her shampoo, her make-up, her perfume, I can see right into the details of her blue irises.

Then Zola appears behind her. He's not dancing. He taps her on the shoulder and walks away and she unclasps me and walks off the floor and into the Control Room with him, leaving me standing there surrounded by her girlfriends who laugh at me. One of them dances towards me, looking at my chest and reaching out her hand. I walk away, climb the stairs and go out into the warm evening.

"Having fun down there were we?" says Andy, smiling sideways at me.

"Going to smoke out here, my break's not over yet," I say, and move away, trying to control my clamouring feelings. The first puff tastes vile and I throw down the cigarette and march back into the club and head down to the Control Room. Zola and Steffi are sitting in the same vat along with three other men. Zola looks at me briefly as I approach and holds out his hand to stop me.

"Wait over there," he says, gesturing with his eyes to a corner of the room. I do as he says and sit on a high barstool in the far corner where I can't see them properly. A minute later Steffi comes out of the vat towing an unknown man by the hand and they disappear through a black door in the back wall. I wait for many minutes more, then Zola comes out of the vat with the other men. As he walks along the vats he looks right through me as if I'm not there, then continues to talk to his companions and exits the Control

Room, leaving me entirely alone, sitting on a stool in the corner. The black door into which Steffi and the man went does not move, even though I watch it for ages. A constant thudding sound is coming down the passage from the dancing pit.

In the passage I come face to face with the Master.

"Aydin, Aydin, they told me you were waiting for me here, I've got a job for you, come back in," and he grasps my arm and leads me back to the vat. As he sits he sighs deeply, looks at the floor for a few seconds then looks up at me with mischievous eyes.

"You're going to love this one. Listen, some snake owes Zola's friend ten grand and I told him – I told him: Aydin's your man, he knows what to do now, just wait 'till you see him, he'll pick that debt up no problem, eh?" and he pats my arm, his eyes drilling into me.

"I'd rather not thanks," I say.

"Rather not?" says the Master loudly, leaning back and looking horrified, his mouth open in astonishment. "Rather not?" he shouts. "What do you think this is? Are beggars choosers now?" Then he slams his hand on the table and I jump. Two empty glasses fall over and clink together. "No no, Aydin," he continues, calming down, "you've got to be strong," and he slaps my arm again but looks serious. "Listen, you go to Kreuzberg next Wednesday morning, that's your patch right? Here's the address," and he produces an envelope from inside his jacket and thrusts it into my hand. "No silly stuff now, you're not a fucking cardboard crusher any more, and don't come back without the ten grand. Got it? Zola'll give you ten per cent," and he stands up and leans over me, placing his ruptured knuckles on the table and looking down at me, his pigtail flopping over his massive shoulder. "Good I got you work, huh?"

"Yeah," I say.

"That's more like it!" and he sits back down and smiles. "Back you go to the door then," and he sits and waits, looking at nothing in particular while I get up and leave.

Wednesday comes round and I'm standing in the urban circus that is Kottbusser Tor. It's not even five blocks from my parents' flat. Big streets all meet here and across them strides a hundred-year-old arched U-Bahn structure that carries trains overhead to and from the city centre. Graffiti is everywhere. This place is the plughole of Berlin and all the dregs go down it. Turks. Kurds. Croatians. Italians. Germans. Punks with pit bulls. Anarchists. Students. And now there are East Germans zipping across the junction in their rat-a-tat two-stroke Duroplast cars.

The name in the envelope claws at me: Mr N. Gökalp. Definitely Turkish. What if he knows me? What if? What if? But just go there, get the money nicely and collect your thousand. The place is above a Turkish eatery; some familiar-looking people give me a friendly wave from inside as I pass by the big window. I buzz the little door to the side and turn to face away from the eatery so they can't see me.

"Gökalp?" says the intercom.

"Postman," I reply. The lock buzzes.

I clump up a wooden staircase so narrow that two men couldn't pass in it. It smells musty and the thin stairs creak. There are two doors at the top and a few shoes on mats on the landing. One door is already open. My heart's in my temples again and I force myself to run the last few steps. He's there waiting for me; he has a gaunt face with eyes sunken unreasonably far either side of a pronounced hook nose on which sit small, round spectacles. He is unshaven; mats of black hair on his head point backwards and upwards and sideways. I see a thin, pallid, hairy arm within a sloppy checked shirtsleeve rolled up. He watches me for a few seconds then his face grows anxious.

"Who are you?" he says in German. Then he utters a cry – "No!" – and he retreats and slams the door. Bolts and chains rattle as I reach the top of the stairs and try to push it open.

I hammer on the door. It's made of thin stuff.

"Gökalp open up, don't make it hard for yourself."

Silence, except for the sounds of the street coming up the stairs. I press and prod at the door a bit. I would prefer to barge it open with my shoulder but there's no run-up space, the landing's too small, so I stand back and give it my hardest kick in the middle. My foot goes right through two thin sheets of chipboard and remains lodged there, leaving me hopping on the doormat. Getting my foot out's difficult.

Through the hole I can see parts of a dirty apartment.

This time I stand further back and aim a side kick near the lock. The second kick makes a vertical crack. The third opens the door. Dust and splinters fly everywhere. I make my way into the flat, which smells of fried breakfast. There's a sound in the kitchen and there he is, clutching a broad chopping knife and quivering in fright.

"I've come for Zola's friend's ten grand."

"I haven't got it!" he says in a high-pitched voice, waving the knife before his eyes and shrinking down into the corner.

"Listen, I'm going to start trashing your apartment. Okay?"

He just stares at me. I don't feel much like doing anything to him but I force myself to sweep the pots and pans from his stove onto the floor, sending food flying, and he jumps in terror and tries to hide behind his knife.

"Give me some money," I make myself shout, "so I can leave you alone, right?"

He's gone silent and just watches me. I grab the heavy wooden kitchen table and heave it over onto its side. A cup and bowl smash and more greasy food runs down a dirty wall.

Then there are voices from out on the stairs.

"Nevzat?" says one voice.

"You okay?" says another in Turkish.

"No!" cries Nevzat Gökalp.

Outside the kitchen I'm confronted by two men, one of them I know from the eatery. They stare at me and I push between them and leave.

"You're fucking useless!" shouts Benjamin Lok. Zola's club is silent and empty. So this is what it's like in the day. "Come with me." I follow him out of the Control Room and into the pit. Without dry ice and dancers it looks and smells like an abandoned warehouse; its black daubing is like glue.

We drive too fast through the town in his growling, tinted-window sports car and he doesn't say a word. At Kottbusser Tor he pulls up by the eatery where they're shutting up shop.

"Get out," he orders.

He goes to the eatery and bangs on the window; I stand a few yards off, frozen in fear. They wave him away and keep on with their cleaning. He stares through the window then bangs again, harder, shaking the whole pane.

A man of solid Anatolian proportions saunters up to the door and shouts in bad German: "Closed now friend. No more food."

The Master marches to his car, opens the boot and

takes out a black baseball bat and returns to the window, ready to swing. I can't tell whether he's really angry or just putting it on.

"Open or I'll smash your shitty shop up, starting with you."

There are shouts and scurrying inside the eatery, like he's kicked an ants' nest. Two other men appear from the back kitchen, making four: two big teenagers, one who I vaguely know, an old man and the other man I know, who's got a meat cleaver. The old man's got a kebab skewer. They approach the door.

"What you want?" shouts the old man defiantly, tilting his head back. He's the only one who doesn't look afraid.

"Here, watch," says the Master and he uses the side of his fist to break a windowpane in the shop door, triggering a volley of shouts from inside. Passers-by have stopped at a distance to watch, clutching each other; cars crawl by and eyes ogle.

The Turks almost start fighting each other to open the door; they each seem bent on getting to us first with their knives and skewers. Then the Master reaches through the hole he's made and grabs one of their arms. Two hands grab his and he yanks backwards and down against a piece of glass that's still in the frame. A cry comes from one of the men and a little curtain of red liquid squirts down the glass and collects on the wooden crosspiece in the door, then drips. The man falls back on the floor clutching his arm then the door opens and the three men try to come out but the Master kicks one of them back inside like a plastic toy and follows him straight in, then he goes up to the old man and, shouting, kicks him ferociously in the thigh, which makes him collapse in a grimacing heap on the floor. The Master doesn't hesitate at all. There's a lot more shouting. The two others square off with him with petrified faces.

"Get me Gökalp from upstairs or I'll smash you all." The baseball bat dangles in his hand. He hasn't even used it.

"We don't know where Gökalp is. What's he got to do with us?"

"I know he's your tenant, don't fuck around with me. Unlock his flat now or I'll mess you up and smash your shop up too."

They're all silent for a moment then the old man speaks from the floor.

"How much he owes?"

"Tell him Aydin," says the Master.

I stutter. They all stare at me. The old man looks calmly at me from the floor. I know he recognises me. I tell him: "Ten thousand deutschmarks."

"Pay them what we've got in the back," says the old man, waving one of the teenagers to go into the back of the shop.

"What?" says one in Turkish, aghast. "Why should we pay his debts? Let's unlock the flat and let him pay."

"Do it!" barks the old man.

We leave with eight thousand six hundred deutschmarks.

"Why so silent?" asks the Master at the wheel. "You think we shouldn't've done that? Huh?" He looks at me and back at the road. "Taken from them? Huh? – Huh?" He's bristling. "Gökalp's their tenant. He owes them money too, fucking gambling lowlife loser. Now he just owes them more. What's wrong with that? What does it matter who he owes it to?" He shoots me more sideways glances. I'm shaking. I can't wait to get away.

"Cheer up Aydin," he laughs as we drive along by the canal, its trees rushing by. "Here," and, steering with his knees, he pulls out the wad of notes and counts me eight hundreds, slapping them into my chest. "You take this. 'Don't worry, be happy!'" I hold the notes to my chest and stare out at the darkening street as we weave between slower cars.

Back home I lock myself in my room. I can't think straight. Hours ooze by. Then the next morning I wander out onto the street beneath a white sky and up Kottbusser Damm, passing beneath the awnings of bakeries, past electrical cabinets plastered with peeling posters of beckoning bikinis, past great glass shop windows advertising sales. When I get to Kottbusser Tor, I spy on the eatery from afar, looking through an arch in the railway bridge. They've already boarded up the hole and the shop is closed.

I want to go and check on the two injured men, but I can't. I even start wanting to go to the mosque just to see people and maybe work out what to do, but I can't go there either, they might be there and they would recognise me. Word might have gone around about the younger of the Mesüt boys. By the afternoon I feel desperate so I go early to karate: maybe I can just train. During the class the Master says nothing to me, doesn't even look at me. Afterwards I force myself to ask him whether he has any work in the gym.

"Work? Here? Aydin! Don't waste your time, you're in the big league now, you can't be a cleaner and wash floors. Come and see me on Friday at Zola's, okay?" He gives me a friendly slap on the shoulder and smiles.

"And Aydin," he calls as I leave, beckoning me back, then lowering his voice, glancing around and leaning in close. "Listen, sorry about what happened. It was wrong of me. Okay?" He puts his hand on my shoulder; it feels affectionate but he also squeezes strangely hard. "I shouldn't have taken you there to your home turf and I shouldn't have hurt those men." He looks into my eyes expectantly and I'm all confusion. "Okay? I'm sorry. Come to Zola's. You can see Steffi. Okay?"

Friday night. Break time has arrived and I go straight into the club. The same music is playing like every week and many of the same people are dancing in the pit. I arrive at the Control Room and Steffi gets up from a vat alone as if she's been waiting for me, comes straight up to me, puts her arms around my neck, puts her face close to mine, holding my eyes with hers, filling me with her perfume and says, "Want to come with me?"

"There's no time, I'm on my break."

She laughs and flicks her hair. "Come on!" she whispers, then she leads me by the hand, around the vats and to the black door where she went last week with the other man. We go down a muffled plywood corridor and into a room with no door but a gauze curtain and whose floor is one big mass of cloths and Persian carpets and cushions and mattresses and candles and water pipes.

I go in. She pulls me to the floor and wraps herself around me, kissing me, making me hot. I feel like someone else. She takes my clothes off. All the things I've so long imagined start happening. I do what I've seen done on late-night TV. She instigates every move, I await surges of emotion, but although my body half-responds, I don't feel much. I act out the feelings just to be on the safe side, including a big climax. I am a good actor. When it's all over she lights a cigarette and blows smoke, but she's just lying there, propped up on her elbow, turned away from me, saying nothing. I touch her shoulder and she doesn't respond, which makes me shiver, and for a long time she keeps looking away at something on the far side of the room and I begin to sense a sadness hanging in the smoky air. I feel I should love her, but I just feel numb. After more silence she says in a quiet voice that I had better go back to my shift.

The Control Room is empty. I am a rudderless boat. I want to wash off what just happened and rewind things with Steffi. Back outside Andy says nothing about my being so late, which means he must be in on it. They all must be in on it. So I just get on with the shift, feeling unclean. Late in the night when most of the people have left, the Master arrives in a different car and greets us without smiling as he goes in; he looks troubled. Later Zola comes out and without any introduction says to me:

"Can you drive?"

"Yes," I say, which is partly true.

"Okay. Come here on Monday morning at eleven. I've got a job for you," and he leaves without waiting for an answer.

4

But the next night is Saturday and it's tournament night. I was selected to fight. This place is packed full of shouting and drinking. The atmosphere's thick and they're playing heavy metal music about death. In the crowd I run into Lars the wiry young doctor; he's carrying a sports bag and his brow is furrowed, his eyes survey the crowd suspiciously. He says nothing. Then we see Mario in tight jeans and a black shirt with white buttons, the top few of which are undone to reveal a gold pendant on a thick golden chain lying against the bulges of his shaven bodybuilder's chest. He's carrying an oversized plastic cup half-full of flat beer.

"Not fighting, Mario?" asks Lars.

"Me? Naa! Hurt my finger," and Mario holds up

his middle finger in Lars' face. He laughs and flashes his even white teeth. "Come!" He leads us to a locker-room. Inside, he hands us some soft, shiny red shorts with golden embroidery around their thick belt-bands.

"What's this?" demands Lars, holding up the garment in disgust. "I've got my gi here, I don't need these," and he tosses the shorts back at Mario's chest.

"Lars," hisses Mario, "this is a Muay Thai contest, you've gotta wear them."

"Muay Thai? I don't fight Muay Thai, don't even know the rules. I fight karate," says Lars. They stare at each other, not saying anything, then Lars picks up his bag. "Bye Mario. Bye Aydin," and he pushes past Mario and leaves.

"What a loser," says Mario. I'm still clutching the colourful shorts.

"There's a thousand marks for winning any fight here and five thousand if you get through to the final. You're in aren't you?"

I nod and begin to change, but I can't stop thinking about Lars. How can he just say no to something without thinking it over? How can he walk away from money like that? Mario helps me get my gloves on and chats about this and that. I can't believe how he can just talk and talk.

"Okay Aydin, you can stay here, I'll come and get you when you're on."

Once Mario's gone, the locker-room is quiet and I feel relieved in his absence; I think he's already a bit drunk. There are pipes running up the wall and no windows in here at all, just bare strip lighting that buzzes. Against one wall are four battered, grey metal lockers, against another there are three blue overalls hanging on pegs. It smells of unwashed clothing and paint. I sit on a slatted bench and watch a fly scuttling hesitantly along a fluorescent light. Time ticks by then the door opens and in bursts the Master with Mario in tow.

"Aydin! Looking good as a Thai fighter! Good boy! You're up next. Don't worry about anything, you'll be just fine as long as you keep your guard up. I'll tell you the rules. Don't worry, be happy!"

I cower there on the bench and the Master stands over me.

"No headbutting and no biting. Otherwise you can do anything you want. Okay? But don't hit them in the groin on purpose. Okay? And don't fall down. This is an exhibition tournament, understand? It's just two rounds then you're done. Normally it's five. Real tough. Okay?"

I nod.

We come out into the crowd. People look at me, inspecting my trunks and bare torso as I pass. I'm thrilled but I'm scared. We wait by the ring for quite a long time – I don't know why. Then we climb up into it, the three of us. Mario is smiling and calling out and waving to all sorts of people he knows. He's got a holdall in his hand. There's a tall woman in a tiny, sky-blue bikini and high-heels, strutting around the ring;

she smiles at me a few times.

The music has changed to something oriental and mystical with hypnotic chimes, like a snake charmer's music. It's a steaming jungle in here. The crowd is all cat-calls, shouts and chanting; the spotlights dazzle me and I can't see the people properly; they're just faces upon faces in the dark.

My opponent clambers in. He's African, blue-black oily skin with muscles like knotted eels. Our eyes meet momentarily; his look like two deep holes in his head. The referee brings us together and says some words but I've already locked onto what's about to happen so I don't hear. The crowd has become white noise in my ears.

Then a bell rings. The fighter stands strangely: different from me, like a praying mantis, his elbows drawn into his ribs, eyes staring out from between blue leather gloves, forearms vertical, one foot raised like a show horse, knee bent ready to do something. He moves cautiously in. Me, I stand as the Master's taught us, like I've done in the dojo a thousand times, and I clench my fists so hard my arms shake. We circle each other, closer and closer. His crazed stare makes me feel sick so I look at his throat instead. There are some strings tied to his upper arms.

Then everything becomes fast and there are slapping noises. I hit him and he hits me, he kicks and knees me and I feel my body shuddering with impacts and hear the noise of leather on skin and the thuds of abdomens and shins. There is no pain except in the distance.

The crowd bays and boos and groans. He comes again and I let him do some things, I shift backwards, absorbing some hits. He's hitting my gloves mainly – quickly, lightning fast, but he's only hitting my gloves and arms like the Master says you never should. He uses his knees too but can't get close enough to get me much. Just a glancing blow or two. I try a front kick to his stomach and he all but runs away. I'm panting hard and he's panting harder. We go around like that for a time and I soon feel like my lungs are going to burst.

Then the bell rings and the referee sends me back to my corner. Mario's there.

"You're losing Aydin, you're not doing anything!"

"What?"

"You've got to do something, he's scoring points and you're not, even if he's not hurting you."

"Okay."

"You've got to do something, you can't just defend, okay?"

"He's nothing. He's just hitting my gloves."

"That's more like it, go get him."

"Where's the Master?"

"He's watching you Aydin, he's watching. Finish this guy off, come on."

"Okay."

My breath is back. The bell goes.

"Just one more round," announces the referee as

the bikini girl climbs out through the ropes. I look at her as she bends.

My opponent comes flying out all fists and knees. His knee gets me properly this time in the thigh. His punches are all over my gloves.

I hop away, my thigh's burning. He's following me. I'm waiting for something to happen but I don't know what. I can't think clearly. I square with him again then he kicks me in the same place on my thigh and juts out his chin to provoke me. What? I lash out at him with a low kick but it misses. The crowd bawls and jeers. He's coming back. I sight up his head then bombard it with fists. My mind is far away. All I can think about is breaking open his head, getting right into his brain matter. His gloves are up, he's moving backwards. I jump on him and grab his head, gloves and all, then jump my knee up into the depths of his stomach and shout out. I become aware of the worried referee nearby. People are shouting everywhere. His left hand moves away from his sagging head so I fire my elbow at his temple.

What I remember is how he falls onto the rubber-matted floor without putting out his hands, like an abandoned marionette. I try to go to him to see if he's alright but they pull me away, raising my glove into the alcoholic air. There's jeering and cheering and a cacophony of shouting. My elbow is in pain. The naked bikini woman circles around me and Mario, looking at my torso. They usher me from the ring and I follow

Mario through the thick crowd, many of whom slap my bare back and make comments.

I'm sitting on the bench in the quiet locker-room feeling my bruises; my elbow's swollen and throbbing like mad. Mario keeps telling me I did fantastic and knocked the guy out. I ask if the man's alright but he tuts dismissively then he says he'll get the Master and he leaves. I feel chilly and my elbow hurts a lot. Nobody comes for a long time and my whole body begins to shake with aftershock. Then I can't stand waiting any more so I go out in the crowd only to meet Mario coming in to get me. He shouts above the din.

"Get dressed, the Master wants to see you."

"I thought there's another fight?"

"No, it's off."

"Do I get my money for winning?"

"Go and get changed then come to the ringside, the Master's there."

I do as he says. The Master is sitting in the front row at the ringside deep in conversation while the crowd shouts and bays, watching another fight that's about to start between a hulking German and a hairy Turk but the Master's not paying attention to that. Then in the row behind him I see Zola sitting with Steffi; she waves and smiles at me. Zola looks right through me. I feel a surge and want to go and take her away, but instead I stand near the Master and wait. The fight has started up in the ring: they're dancing around and bludgeoning each other. People shout at me to sit down and get out of the way, so I kneel by the Master and he glances at me but keeps talking.

Steffi and Zola are leaving; I see he's got a grip on her arm and I want to follow them and take her away from him but I don't. The Master has finished talking and turns to me.

"So my boy? You did well but why did you wait till the last minute like that?"

"I dunno. Didn't realise how quick the rounds would go."

"There, you see? That's how it is. You have to finish them straight off. When I was fighting I would aim for thirty seconds, maybe one minute. Sometimes it took just fifteen seconds."

He stands and offers me his hand, which I shake.

"Well done though. Shame about the other fight being cancelled. See you Monday."

He starts to leave with Mario. In the ring up above, the Turk is taking a beating against the ropes. I see his hunched, hairy back heaving.

"Master?" I call. He turns and looks at me impatiently.

"Yes?"

"Do I get paid for the fight?"

"Paid? Paid? No, no. That would've been the other fight." He turns away again.

"Mario said there would be a thousand marks for

winning."

"Did you say that?" says the Master to Mario. "Did you say that?" Mario looks as if he wants to protest but he swallows instead. The Master sighs and reaches into his inside pocket. "Here, take this from me personally, you did well," and he counts out five blue notes.

"Thanks."

"You're welcome," says the Master. "You're my fighter, I have to pay you." He turns to make his way out through the crowd, and people shake his hand and slap his back as he disappears into the mass.

The whole next day I feel sore in all sorts of places, but I can only think of Steffi's bronze skin and naked back and blue, crystalline irises. I go over and over what happened in the room with her, not wanting to forget any part of it, adding on feelings which hadn't been there. And I wonder about her sadness.

The evening arrives and I realise I'm looking forward to seeing Zola tomorrow morning and doing whatever job he's got lined up for me. I don't really like him, but I admire him. He's from the East, but not East Berlin – Russia, Hungary, who knows; he obviously came here long before the Wall fell and he's successful, riding above the cares of run-of-the-mill people. Whatever job he has for me might be exciting and now I feel grateful to him for giving me Steffi that night. I feel upbeat. No more department store. The images of the blood in the eatery try to come back but I push them aside with the Master's apology, suspending the fact that I know he didn't mean it.

Feeling high, I run all the way down to Abgang hoping to see Slobodan and there he is, inside at a table, talking to the drug dealer Wolfgang the Pigtail, whom I've never seen actually sitting down and who stands up as I arrive and greets me with a formal smile and a firm shake of the hand. Slobodan looks obliquely at me and I can tell they're in the middle of talking so I excuse myself and go out back to give them time to finish, but I'm too excited to stay away for long. When I return, Wolfgang has disappeared.

"Scoring a hit?" I ask. Slobodan winces at my puerile comment and I blush.

"What's got into you," he says, "coming here on a Sunday night. You not working tomorrow?"

"No. No," I say breathlessly. "I'm not working at the department store any more. I'm working for Zola. Driving for him."

"What?" he says, aghast, eyes wide.

"So? It's good. I've already earned a thousand marks."

"Just driving?" he says, disbelievingly.

"Yeah," I lie. Don't want to mention the eatery.

Slobodan says nothing and looks at me carefully. Then Wolfgang reappears wearing his leather biker's jacket and smiling, making creases that radiate out from the side of each eye. He has completely straight hair dragged back in a pigtail that hangs right down his back, like the Master's, only longer and greasier.

"Bye fellas," he says, making to leave, but Slobo stops him.

"Aydin says he's driving for Zola on Ku'damm now, making a thousand marks a shot," says Slobodan.

Wolfgang's face goes smooth. He scrutinises me expertly. Then he simply knocks on the table and leaves.

"You see that Aydin?" hisses Slobodan once he's gone. "You see? He knows what shit you get into. He knows Zola. Zola's not a good man, Aydin."

"It's better than crushing rubbish for a living," I say, dragging Slobo's tobacco packet towards me, hoping to return to our usual banter.

"I'm worried for you. You mustn't get mixed up with the likes of Zola. And who got you the job? Your karate master? It's not good, Aydin. These are bad people." His Serbian accent is coming out.

"Anyway let's not talk about it," I reply. "I got laid on Friday."

"Oh yeah?" he says, his tone changing. "She nice?"

"Totally stunning. She just grabbed me and took me into this room. It was amazing."

"Where?"

"At Zola's."

"A room? Fuck, brother, I told you. Is it a brothel now as well?"

"Don't be rude," I say, the heat rising in my face. "They just have this room, it's not public or anything."

"I should hope not."

We laugh. I feel sick to the stomach but I need his friendship.

One more beer then I take my leave; Slobo stays to drink.

The next morning at eleven. Zola comes out of his club and hands me the key to an Audi V8 that's parked by the curb.

"Get in and wait."

The car is new but smells strongly of cigarettes and its ashtray is overflowing with butt ends and ash. With a jolt I realise someone is sitting behind and across from me: a pasty, greasy German with mousy hair who shifts in his seat.

"Hello," I say, but he just looks hard out of the window. I glance again in the mirror. His skin has tiny black and red spots as if he might have some kind of illness.

Zola reappears and gets in the back, dragging in a smell of cologne. Another man climbs in next to me. He's very tall, blond and dressed all in black and has to fold himself up to fit in through the door. He slides the chair back abruptly and the German behind him starts and swears.

"Calm down boys," says Zola. "You don't know each other and you don't know me either. Got it?"

The back seat man grunts and the tall blond man nods.

"Got it?" says Zola, tapping my shoulder. "You don't know me."

"Got it."

"Drive. I'll tell you where to go."

We wend our way south through the city and at Schöneberg we stop to let Zola out. He tells me to drive the men down to Dahlem Dorf tube station. On the way they don't say a single word. It's leafy in Dahlem and there's more space between the buildings; there are separate houses and lots of them have big lawns. Students come and go from the underground clasping folders and books under their arms, talking to each other and criss-crossing the neatly cobbled road. A lot of them wear black. There's grass and trees everywhere. One round patch of grass outside the station has a big, colourful flowerbed in the middle and the station itself has a thatched roof like a country cottage.

The others tell me to wait while they go somewhere; I think of asking them what's happening but it seems better not to. There are lots of expensive cars here. Ten minutes later the men reappear and put something in the boot then climb back into the car.

"Drive to Schöneberg. Zola's waiting for us."

Back at the club, Zola pays me five hundred marks – a whole week's wages in my old job – then says he'll see me Friday night.

I am no longer a department store rubbish packer. I am a driver, a bouncer and a fighter. A deliciously empty week stretches before me and the first thing I do is go earlier than I've ever been to Abgang with a hundred mark note. By the time Slobodan arrives I'm drunk with some people I don't know. The next day I sleep it off in my room then on Wednesday I go again, this time with two hundred marks. We go on to another pub in Neukölln, then we take a tube to Schöneberg and visit a bar I don't know, with plastic tables. I lose count of the drinks we have. Early Thursday morning I find myself lying in the undergrowth at the little park on Bayerischer Platz with no money and my underpants on the wrong way around. People hurry to their morning shifts and eye me suspiciously.

I haven't been to karate all week so I go later that day but feel like throwing up. My head pounds when I jump, my legs feel like they're full of silt. I'm afraid of being hit and my punches don't seem to hurt anyone.

On Friday I go to the mosque and fall fast asleep during the sermon. My father refuses to talk to me but it doesn't matter because I'm just trying to make it through to the evening. When the evening comes at the club, I take my break early, find Steffi on the dance floor and try to kiss her but she fends me off with half a smile and gently says no. But she does slip me her phone number. I try ringing it all day Saturday, but no one answers. On Sunday a man answers and listens to me asking for her, then hangs up. I pace around my tiny bedroom with the curtains closed and the heater on full, sneak out into the carpet corridor when all's quiet, dial the phone again, listen to the long desolate beeps, then slink back to the tepid light of my room and think of her with the mystery flatmate and other men.

Then in the evening she answers and whispers to come on Tuesday night so I do. She lives in Wedding in a bedsit she shares with a male student who's apparently her "friend" and who greets me coolly and leaves. Straight away we take off our clothes. We don't even talk. But afterwards we look into each other's eyes for a long time and laugh, and I feel at home.

Later I leave and wander out into a muted dawn. Images begin to come to me of her flatmate returning to spend the rest of the week there, which makes me want to scream and cry.

By the coming Thursday my money's all spent again. I've not been to karate since last week's failed session. On Friday Zola says he's got another driving job which I say yes to and on Monday it turns out to be just like the last, but to Tegel this time, waiting in the smoky Audi, collecting something, stone dead silence on the way there and back, five hundred deutschmarks in a tiny curled-up cylinder, money I then spend the same way on a week's drinking.

This routine goes on. One day we just drive a little way up Kurfürstendamm, park, and wait. After some time, the men in the back get out as usual, but then they get straight back in again in a hurry and order me to drive away quickly. They both look out of the back window as I move into the traffic. In the rear view mirror I see a police car swerve into the space we were in and officers jumping out, but they run into a shop and my passengers turn back and say nothing. We return to the club by an indirect route and I get paid, but only two hundred deutschmarks.

I see Steffi the next evening and we talk properly for the first time. We discuss music and what we used to like at school, and I tell her about my parents and find myself saying good things about them.

The next Monday I drive the men over the border into East Berlin, along the wide, wide boulevards lined with immense, commanding, bleak buildings, monuments to a state that has just collapsed, and into a down-at-heel residential area called Friedrichsfelde. There are few cars around, most of them East German and Czech models. We wait for a long time outside a sad-looking sports field where some youths are playing football and a man in a blue tracksuit is running round and round the track. Some skinheads sauntering along the pavement give our car a slap and a kick as they pass and I make to get out but my companions stop me.

"Don't be stupid, Aydin. It's dangerous here," says the tall blond man in black.

In my wing mirror I watch the skinheads getting

smaller and kicking other cars. And they barge an elderly man off the pavement. Some time later a man in an anorak appears nearby and loiters at a lamp post, and my passengers get out and talk to him, exchange something with him, then return to the car and we drive away.

I do driving jobs like this every week. The days are strung out in a green haze, one week rolled into the next, driving, boozing and sleeping, wandering the streets, sniffing Wolfgang the Pigtail's lines at Abgang, buzzing, standing on weekend evenings outside the club, driving to odd parts of Berlin on Mondays, Steffi's flat on Tuesday nights, Friday nodding off at the mosque for my father's sake, round and round in a spiral, hoping on the next job and the next Tuesday night, listening to the same music behind the drawn curtains of my room.

It's another Monday, but today Zola climbs in the back of the Audi and the Master in the front. The other men don't show up. The Master slaps my thigh but says nothing and stares ahead. Zola says: "Kreuzberg," so I drive. We drive up to Tiergarten and along Strasse 17 Juni, through the park where people amble and cycle the criss-cross pathways; then around the Siegessäule with its golden angel statue high up on top, gazing out over the grey city beneath an overcast sky; then on towards the Brandenburg Gate. Most of the Wall there has been removed and I can see people wandering around among the debris and dust. Vendors have set up stalls, carts and hot-dog trailers in what used to be the Death Strip. I shiver. Berlin felt safer when the Wall was up.

When we get to Kreuzberg, Zola directs me to an address near my parents' flat.

"Come, Aydin," says the Master, getting out. "We may need you for this."

We all enter an old courtyard a bit like the one in my parents' tenement, but here litter lies around an unkempt garden and a cat trots away between dirty bins. At the far side of the yard is a door with a crack in its glass pane, which the Master pushes open, leading into a dark stairwell. Zola slaps the light switch and turns the stairwell a dim yellow.

We tramp up the creaking stairs to the fourth floor, where the Master signals me to stand to one side of a brown door while he stands to the other. The place smells of cat urine.

Zola rings the buzzer. Soon the peephole flickers and Zola holds up a plastic carrier bag in front of it for the occupant to see.

The door opens and Zola marches in, followed by the Master.

Ahead of them down a short, dark corridor where sundry jackets hang, I see the outline of a short, stocky man with enormous shoulders and slicked-back, receding hair. We enter a living room in disarray. It has a purple carpet and magazines and overflowing ashtrays and stained glasses clutter a glass coffee table in front of a TV.

The man turns to face us.

"Where are your usual boys?" he asks, looking wary. He is Kurdish, I can see that now; and I hear it in his accent. Deeply suspicious eyes flicker between us and he scans me from head to toe from beneath great, bushy brows.

"Who's this?" he demands, waving dismissively at me. "What is this?" he continues, looking angrily at the men, who have not said a word. "You got problem?"

"Just get the parcel, Yez," commands Zola.

"Show me money," demands Yez.

Zola holds the plastic bag open and Yez peers in, then turns and disappears into what looks like a bedroom and returns holding a parcel the size of a big bag of flour, bound up with brown sticky tape.

"Sit," he says sullenly, pointing to the sofas. "Show me money."

"We're not sitting," says Zola.

Yez freezes, clutching his parcel. "What is this? You got problem?"

The Master walks around the sofa so he's standing behind him.

"Give me money!" shouts the frightened, angry Kurd.

"There's no money for cheats, Yez," says Zola.

A cat appears and jumps effortlessly up onto the

back of the sofa, looking up hopefully at its angry owner.

"Oh look," says Zola, picking up the cat, which turns to him and mews hopefully. "Your pet cat."

"Leave him!" cries Yez.

Zola walks over to an open window. "Bye-bye pussy," he says casually, and tosses the cat straight out. There is a long silence, then a distant smacking sound that echoes up from the courtyard.

Yez emits a strangled shriek.

"Hand over the parcel," says Zola. "And never give me half measures again, otherwise you'll be following pussy."

Yez is shaking with incandescent rage but says nothing. He slowly hands the parcel to Zola, but when Zola takes it, he holds on.

"I get you back. I get you back," he hisses through clenched teeth, his eyes ringed with anger, ablaze with pent-up fury. "I get you back. I get you back." He glances at the Master, who stands there menacingly, then at me. "You as well, Turkish," and he points a stubby, hairy finger at me and looks right into my eyes. "I never forget face. I seen you around here. I know you. I kill you all."

We leave him standing there and clump down the dark stairwell. Zola slaps a light switch half way down and the yellowness returns. As we cross the yard, I lock my eyes on the Master's back so as not to catch sight of the dead cat, but I see it in the corner of my vision.

I'm returning home that same evening. Everywhere I see faces, and there are many Kurds. Much more than I ever thought. Along our street I see at least two, and they look at me as I pass. I look as far ahead as I can, scanning for anyone short and stocky with big shoulders. When I get near my entrance, I break into a jog, slip in through the door and run up the stairs to see whether my parents are alright.

The next Monday I drive Zola's car to Treptow in the East, but this time the usual men are with me again, sitting in silence. When we arrive I wait at a parking lot near the Soviet memorial, adding to the stuffed-full ashtray, enwrapped in blue smoke, when my accomplices come running from behind. Both doors open, sending my blue cloud into a dance.

"Drive. DRIVE!"

I drive. The wailing is distant at first but it catches up quickly, a swarm of blue lights in the rear-view mirror. At a red traffic light we get stuck and can't drive anywhere so we all burst out of the car and run in different directions. There's so much shouting I just run. When the barking and snarling starts up behind me I get scared. Then my running slows down, my lungs are tearing apart, my legs are saying no. But I run on, alongside the black river now. Behind me a tearing snapping sound mingles with the barking and shouting.

"Stop!" comes a shout. "Police! We've caught your mates."

Then I jump off a low wall into the black river. Under the water it's brown and cold and silent.

But I have to come up. Something is hurting my arm. I call out, swallowing oily soily water. There's so much splashing. Then out of the water comes a dark fanged muzzle and it bites my face and rips something off my eye. I grab at that hairy muscular snapping thing and it grabs me back ten times harder driving ivory nails into my hand.

"I give up!" I shout, flailing my arms. "I give up!"

"Off! Off!"

The water is smooth again and I'm standing in mud. My shoes are lost. Two black seals are swimming gracefully to the bank powered by their tails. When they climb out they shake off the water.

Six human silhouettes are standing on the low riverside wall against the skyline; I cannot see their faces. They're wearing police caps on their heads and items on their belts, two have other dogs straining at leashes. Warm blood is in my mouth with the mud. Then one of the figures speaks in a commanding, kind voice:

"Come in now, we'll not hurt you as long as you don't fight. Come on. It's over. Come."

So I drag myself up through the mud and commit myself to their mercy.

PART II

5

Everything echoes in here. Baboon calls and parrot shrieks bounce down varnished white hard stone corridors until dusk, until one after the other the inmates settle on their roosts and fall quiet. Then at 10.27 p.m. comes the soft tramp of the warder going by. The lights go out and things in my mind begin to echo. Then there are noises that come from the neighbouring rooms. Bumps. Groans. Radios. Snoring. Crying. Shrill laughter. Then it's 5.30 a.m. and the lights come back on.

This is the reason why my head droops and my eyelids feel so leaden when I sit at the table sorting capacitors out and into a tray, plastics in a bin, batteries in another bin, cables over there. We dismantle old computers and household appliances.

"Fuckin' slave labour," according to my table mate Jörg Kleemann. He's here for setting his pit bull on, kicking and urinating on a policeman who was evicting him from a squat in Prenzlauer Berg, a district in the middle of East Berlin where certain kinds of Westerners are fast moving in: non-conformists, anti-fascists and all kinds of alternative types.

Me, I see it differently: I'm glad they give us work here. They even pay us for it, which to my mind is odd. Not that it's much money; just a nominal amount which we can spend at an over-priced, under-stocked shop that sells things that gather dust: Russian chewing gum, bland, stale crisps, magazines from last year or the year before and single-ply toilet roll in opened packets.

I'm sitting and sorting. I like to do it fast.

"What you rushing for? Slavin' labour for capitalists." Jörg tosses a cable into my plastics bin and I remove it without comment and place it back on the desk.

"They're profiting from us here, brother. People are suing big corporations for using slave labour under the Nazis but here we are, the new slaves. You've got to emancipate yourself my brother." He retches and spits something gelatinous onto the floor. I shift my chair away an inch; he comes across as permanently unwell. His hair is caked with grease and there are puss-filled swellings around some of his ear studs. He must once have been athletic; you can still see the remnants of strong musculature. His eyes are sky-blue and wet with a milky liquid. He has a spherical stud in his tongue and a pin through his lower lip, and when he drifts away, slouched backwards staring, he clicks them together out of habit, then sucks in drool when he returns to awareness. There is eczema all over his stunted hands; when he leaves his station I sometimes see flakes of scab and skin lying on his sorting mat.

"It's against my fuckin' human rights," he says. "Against our fundafuckinmental rights."

"You're fundafuckinmental," I say.

Jörg tuts and goes quiet.

Later I ask him, "Do you do drugs?"

"Naa. Not now."

Me, I do. Well they're not really drugs, they're just little white pills that Marlowe Grünwald slips me at breakfast. He's creepy but he's okay. I admit he scares me with his bulging eyes; they project so far out of his skull, you can see the side of his eyeball when you look at him from the side. His skeleton wheels the trolley of dirty dishes. He works in the kitchen, which is how he knows me and everyone, because he brings the food to our dining stations and takes away the dishes, and on my very first day he took a liking to me and started slipping me a pill.

I take it after breakfast, secretly. It's a bit like being drunk, but not quite: everything goes a bit liquid, my limbs tingle and go numb, everything becomes molten for a while until lunchtime, then it fades and prison comes back. My lawyer told me I might be out in a year or so because I was unaware, I didn't know what I was driving for, what we were collecting and dropping off. The prosecutor said I must have known, or should have known, should have asked, and that in any case not knowing is no excuse.

The judge sent me here and told me I was wasting my life and should better myself. I can't see how I can better myself here but at least with these pills I can keep going and keep my head down. My parents didn't come to court because mother got ill and wasn't allowed to feel stressed. My uncle came and he visits me every week and tells me news. But what I look forward to most is the morning pill.

I'm in the yard. It's a dry football pitch where we play. Frank Lordowski and his gang usually walk straight across our game, provoking. Mostly nothing happens but there was a fight once and he beat a man almost to death, sitting on him and punching, punching. Whenever we tried to get him off, his clique pushed us away and called us scum. You could see the victim's bone where the skin came off all around his eye-socket. I'd never seen a skull before. Lordowski's giant knuckles were covered with blood and grit so you couldn't read the tattoos on them, his green eyes were squinting with rage, darting at us from his great, shaven, scar-nicked cranium; but then he seemed strangely amiable in the aftermath like a monster sated after devouring its prey, looking at me and almost saying something.

Today as he and his hangers-on pass by, one of them calls me a Turkish dog. Jörg Kleemann wants to spit at them but another man stops him. I wish I could be Lordowski's friend and not a friend of Jörg Kleemann. It's the afternoon. Thoughts of the next morning pill are in my head. When the pill wears off I feel pain, but not bodily; a dull pain in my imagination. Then from across the yard a warder calls my name.

"You're late. You've got Woyak at four. Get there now!"

"Woyak, Woyak, go and cry to Woyak," chants an inmate who I don't know. I skulk away.

Adelbert Woyak's room would be the nicest room in the prison but it has no windows. A solitary table-top lamp casts its cone of yellow light on an armchair whose armrests have been worn through to the stuffing at the ends where your hands go. I pick there too, pulling out tufts and smoothing down up-springing threads when I don't know how to answer his questions.

"Why do you think afternoons are worse than mornings for you?" – things like that, because if I tell the truth about the pills he'll set off an investigation and I'll stop getting the pills and make an enemy of Marlowe Grünwald.

His eyes are moist and there are little creases at

the corners, glistening behind taped-together reading glasses. A whirring noise comes from an extractor fan and I smell mildew, but at least the room is warm.

"Do you feel sad in the afternoon?" – things like that too: do I feel sad? Do I feel sad? I had a session with Woyak in the morning once and giggled all the way through; he eyed me disapprovingly and made copious notes on his pad with his little soft hand, the hand I dislike having to shake. Hasn't anyone told him his moustache looks like Hitler's? Perhaps Lordowski likes him; his friends go on about Hitler all the time. But Adelbert Woyak would not have fared well under Hitler: he is kind, delicate and interested in young men's troubles.

"How would you describe your relationship with your father?" he says, pad on lap, looking at me over his reading glasses.

"He thinks I'm not religious enough," I reply.

"And what do you think Aydin, are you religious enough?"

"It's not me I'm worried about," I say.

"Who are you worried about Aydin?"

I remain silent and his gentle voice goes on.

"Are you worried about not being religious?"

I look at his stupid glasses. Why doesn't he buy some new ones?

"Is it your father you're worried about?"

I'm still considering the previous question so I just say no.

"Is it God you're worried about?"

My mouth is all clamped up so I say nothing at all and pick at the chair; I feel on edge now. There is a long pause full of whirring.

"Is that something you'd rather not talk about Aydin?"

Part of me wants to spill my guts out to this man; part of me wants to mock him.

"I don't mind," I say, sighing.

Then, when I don't say anything else for a long time he shifts in his seat and says: "Do you think you need help or are you quite alright as you are, doing time here among this lot?" – when he says that, I stand up suddenly and look down on him and say: "I don't need help from you," then walk out.

This isn't a prison where you're locked up in a cell all day long like in films. They say they want us to take responsibility for our lives, so we can move around the complex a lot of the time. Then there's the work: they say the routine is good for us and that earning a little money gives us self-esteem and accustoms us to the realities of a regular life outside.

And we have our own rooms. It's nice in a way. I'm lying in my room now, waiting for the veil of sleep to descend so that the morning can arrive. I'm crossing a lake in a boat. The water is dark black and bubbling like the cauldrons of the underworld. My father has a life jacket; I do not and the boat takes on water and I am sucked down and he looks at me as if he does not know me as I disappear and the water closes in above and I feel it at the gates of my lungs and my heart bursts with blood. My whimpering awakens me. There is a thumping from the next room and somebody shouts.

The grey light of morning has already arrived. Breakfast and the pill in two hours. A gentle rhythmic bumping is coming through the wall now, but it stops eventually.

The canteen at breakfast next day.

"Marlowe," I hiss, as he tries to slip away.

"Marlowe, I need to talk to you."

"What is it Aydin, you've got your pill."

"Can't you get me another one? Two to cover the whole day?"

"Sure Aydin," he whispers. "Fifty deutschmarks. Or I can get you something better for a hundred."

"Okay. Tomorrow, okay? I'll get the money."

I don't have fifty marks, only twenty. At the sorting table I ask Jörg if he has fifty I can borrow.

"Why, for Grünwald? Fuckin' loser fuck."

"None of your business."

"Sure Aydin. I've only got a hundred though. Give me the change."

"Okay. I'll pay you back."

Breakfast next day.

"Marlowe. I've got your money."

"Sorry Aydin, no pills, ran out."

"What?"

"No pills. Unless you've got a hundred, then I can give you something."

I'm so dying for a lift.

"I've got a hundred. What you got?"

"Here," he whispers, slipping me an object wrapped in some tissue. "Hundred marks. Hurry up."

I delve into my pocket and thrust the crumpled note into his chilly, damp hand then go to my seat and try to eat. Everyone around seems to be glancing at me and whispering.

In my room I unwrap the object: it's a syringe with something in it. I put it down and sink my face into my hands. Then I hide the syringe in my cupboard. Later after work I take it out and pull off the thin plastic sheath to reveal the needle. It looks oily. Am I to insert that between the fibres of my muscles, into my vein tube? I touch the tip: it scratches the grooves of my fingerprint like a record stylus. The liquid in the tube is clear but slightly brown. I hide it again. There's no way I'm going to do that.

"Marlowe," I hiss at him the next morning. "I can't use that thing you gave me. Don't you have something I can swallow?"

"No Aydin, no pills," and he moves away with his trolley, stopping at a group of Lordowski's men to talk.

At the sorting table Jörg asks me for his money back. I say I don't have it. I can hardly speak. I notice nothing, everything seems cold. A sound is clicking in my head and my ears ring periodically; something is moving in the fluid of my eye; I rub it but it returns in suspension. I'm cold but sweating a lot and shivering too. Back at my room I get out the syringe and look at it, even apply it to my arm and press it a bit to make a dent, then I wrap it up again and go to the toilet and try to vomit.

The day drips by in a series of deranged images. I go silent on Woyak and he sends me away. Outside in the yard I sit on the sidelines and stare across the pitch. The brick walls stare at me – I could walk through them, climb over them. Would the warders amble up so casually as they did to Lordowski's mangled victim? I imagine myself on the outside but all I can think about there is the syringe I've left behind. All the inmates nod to me one by one. All the warders nod. The walls nod to me one by one.

I walk zombie-like to my room and take out the syringe in a sweat, hearing nothing of the screaming voice. The needle slips in through my skin without pain, pushing up a long hump along my blue vein, then I press the plunger and feel a cold thread climbing up my arm then a burning in my heart; I cry out and fall off a stool; it is the dentist's chair under the laughing gas, it's quite alright here; my vision closes into a tunnel, over whose rim peers the wardrobe and ceiling, talking to me; someone dangles happily from a gibbet beneath the skies of Italy. There are whales and hand-maidens spilling in, their swords flashing. Pleasure engulfs my frame and the words fall away.

6

I don't remember where I went after that, only that
I want to go back. I am hungry. I want to go back to
that world of sloping dreams. At breakfast I want to
go back. Grünwald scorns me when I beg him and say
I have no money; after that, I just want to go back. I
want to go back. I skip lunch as well and crouch in
the corner of my room because the bed and the stool
must not be soiled by contact with me. I just want
to go back. At the yard I'm terrified and somebody
barges me and I turn to face the wall. I need another
hundred from somewhere.

I am not going to wash my body until I can go back.
I need another hundred from somewhere if I want to
go back. Payday: fifty marks. When Jörg's away from
the table I rifle his pockets and find his fifty and go off

in search of Grünwald.

Back at my room I look at the new needle and when protesting voices come I insert it in the same place and have done with them.

It's the next day and I can't come out of my room. I must dispose of the needles first. I must dispose of the needles so that I can go back to the dream world: one more time; all good things come in threes then I'll stop and get back on track. My experimenting days were good but they're over after this one last time. A cleaned-up man will look back and laugh.

At the sorting table, Jörg accuses me of theft but I don't know where he got the idea that I would steal. He says I owe him a hundred and fifty now but I think it's a hundred, maybe less. The more I think about it, the less I think I owe him.

In the yard, Lordowski says something to me as he passes – a greeting – and one of his followers spits at me. I feel only a vague urge to retaliate. It's said around prison that Marlowe Grünwald's ill. I will have to wait.

Four days pass and I'm still waiting for my one last shot before I go clean.

It's the afternoon and we're told to go to the canteen to listen to someone talk to us about voluntary work. We're all there, everyone from our block: Lordowski and his gang all along the back row, everyone else scattered around other plastic seats. People are flicking and kicking each other under the seats, throwing objects, calling out things. Two warders stand in the corners and look at us with grim disdain.

Then in walks a well-dressed man we don't know and everyone goes quiet. As soon as I see him I can't stop looking at him. He must be in his sixties and has floppy white hair; I think he must have combed it earlier but it's starting to go awry. His skin is pink with a sheen, almost leathery; there are lines across his forehead where his hair has receded slightly. His eyes are the bluest I've ever seen and they look out at us. His face is full of something about to happen. He is clean-shaven, and from where I'm sitting I can smell a cologne that throws me to another time. He is wearing a tweed suit. Maybe he's from the countryside and not the city like us. His shirt collar fits snugly around his neck and he's wearing a blue, red and gold diagonally striped tie. All his clothes fit around a trim, alert old body.

Everyone's quiet, but then somebody laughs. Then someone tells the laugher to shut up and another someone tells that person to shut up and there's some whispering and chortling, then silence again. I look at the visitor but still his face does not move, he just scans us, looking from each inmate to the next as if inspecting horses. He has the fingers of one hand spread out on the tabletop where he's standing. I'm actually afraid for him and what they might say, he seems so clean and good. He looks from one man to the other and when he finally looks at me his gaze settles for a moment and I have to look away.

Then he speaks and his voice is much stronger and kinder than I expected.

"Good afternoon gentlemen."

There are scattered replies, mostly mumbles. He smiles.

"My name is Heinrich von Weser. I'm very glad to be able to talk to you today. I come with an invitation."

His German is clear. There is not a single thing wrong with it.

"An invitation?" pipes up Jörg Kleemann from the side of the room. "To your house yeah? I'll come if I can live like you."

I hadn't noticed Kleemann; he doesn't sit near me any more.

"Yes, to my house," replies Heinrich von Weser. Somebody laughs but most people are quiet. Jörg Kleemann tuts scornfully and the white-haired man continues: "You are welcome there. But you have to help me."

"Help you with what? Cleaning your cars?" retorts Kleemann. I wish he would be quiet.

"No, I would like to invite you to help people."

"What, help you? Posh people, yah? Need us for your dirty work, yah?"

The white-haired man looks at him in curious indifference like a doctor examining a symptom. Then he turns away and addresses us all: "There are people less fortunate than me, even less fortunate than you because they do not have long to live. I run a hospice for terminally ill people. I need your help."

Jörg Kleemann has gone quiet at last. But then one of Lordowski's men calls out from the back.

"I know you. Aren't you a bloody count or something?"

The old man chuckles and tucks his thumbs lightly into the pockets of his jacket. "You say that like an accusation," he says, looking evenly at the man.

Then Jörg Kleemann pipes up again in his snide voice: "It is."

There is a pause. "Yes, I am a count, and I am privileged," says Heinrich von Weser. "But there is one privilege we all hopefully share, which is the prospect of a long life. The people in our hospice don't have that and I'm asking you whether you might want to help them in their final months and years."

"Bloody slave driver..." whispers Kleemann under his breath, but we all hear it.

Another of Lordowski's men barks from the back: "It was you and your lot who tried to kill Hitler." Everyone goes quiet again and we look at the visitor nervously.

Heinrich von Weser straightens himself and his smile fades. One of the warders starts making towards the man at the back, but von Weser holds out his hand

and stops him in his tracks. His eyes fix the man at the back. Even the fidgeting has stopped: utter silence. I can't stop looking at him. He has complete command of himself. The warders are in his thrall. Von Weser replies in a measured tone:

"That sounds like an accusation too."

Then Lordowski speaks up in his deep, booming voice we so seldom hear:

"Adolf Hitler was good for Germany. If you tried to kill him, you tried to kill Germany."

Von Weser replies without hesitation. "Is that what you believe?" His tone remains polite. "Aren't you too young to have met Hitler? Or did your father know him?"

"I don't know my father, old man," replies Lordowski.

Von Weser raises his eyebrows. "I see. In any case, we saw it the other way around." He smiles. "What you call 'my lot' believed that if nobody tried to get rid of him, Germany would be destroyed."

Everyone's silent. Then von Weser says: "Perhaps we can continue with the hospice?"

I'm thinking to myself: "Don't bother asking their permission, just tell them to shut up," but he waits for an answer, then when nobody replies he turns to his overhead projector and switches on some slides of his hospice and some of the patients there, as well as some young men like us serving food and wheeling people around the grounds in wheelchairs. One of the patients is a child with no hair and a purple scalp – cancer, I guess – but he's smiling at something.

When Heinrich von Weser is finished and gone I sit there, the last to leave the canteen. Everyone else has gone out to the yard but I stay put in case Heinrich von Weser comes back in; maybe he might. I look to see if he left anything. When he doesn't come back, I go over to where he was standing and smell his cologne. Then I go outside but straight away the sight of the inmates playing football unsettles me and I go to my room and begin to cry into my plastic pillow for a long time until I can't cry a single tear more, even though I try. Then I want to go to supper but I'm too afraid of seeing my fellow inmates in the state I'm in. The next day I have a fever. The doctor comes; he smells of korn schnapps like I used to drink at Abgang. The next day I go to see Woyak but I can't say anything. I can only think about the white-haired man and Grünwald. As soon as Grünwald gets back and I've done my last shot I'm going to sign up for von Weser's hospice.

Jörg Kleemann is no longer working with me. In his place is Breuniger, one of Lordowski's boys, tall but barely out of adolescence; he would be handsome if it weren't for a rigid quality to his looks. His face has only three expressions – amazement, disdain and self-satisfaction – between which he shifts without apparent reason. His hair is shaved up the back and sides and perfectly combed on top.

Two days after his arrival at my sorting table he whispers – unnecessarily, since nobody can hear us – that Lordowski wants to see me that afternoon. He seems to enjoy withholding the reason why.

In the yard they're waiting for me in a semi-circle around Lordowski. I can tell some of his boys hate me and are only pretending to tolerate me.

Lordowski's green eyes look down onto the top of my head: I have to tilt my head back just to meet them. Everything about him is larger than you'd think possible: his lips like great stuffed, dried-up earthworms, his crooked teeth, his thick, veined neck like one of my thighs. When I stand face to face with him it's his neck I'm looking at right in front of my eyes, and on it, either side, are two arteries that pulse slowly.

As he begins to speak I smell his breath.

"They tell me," he says in a carnivorous voice, "you're a fighter."

"No," I reply.

"Oh." He licks his great lips and looks at the side of my eye, as if examining some blemish there. "Shame, because if you were I'd have five hundred marks for you."

"Why?"

"Don't ask why, boy," he says. "If you prove you're a tough guy like they say you are and I can rely on you,

134

we'll all look after you, won't we boys? You can be our little Turk. I know you need things…"

He looks at me, as do his men, who chortle darkly.

"What do I have to do?"

"You kick the living daylights out of Woyak. Hospitalise him. No half-jobs."

"Why don't you do that yourself? You can do it better."

Frank Lordowski's friends go nervously quiet and he takes a step even closer to me so that I can feel the heat radiating from his chest and neck and smell his odour puffing out from his shirt top.

"Do you want to join us or just float on your fuckin' own?"

"I'll do it if you give me a hundred marks in advance," I say, thinking of the needle. "To prove you're going to pay."

Lordowski steps back and laughs, looking around at his gang members.

"Desperate for our next hit are we? Got the shakes?"

They all chuckle.

"Give him a hundred," says Lordowski.

A short, fat man with a shaven head holds out a note but as I'm about to take it he drops it to the floor and stares at me.

I hesitate and look first at him, then Lordowski, but Lordowski is looking across the yard.

I stoop to the floor to get the note, expecting a blow on the back of my head or a kick in the face, but instead I just feel their loathing pouring onto me as I crouch. The note is moist with the fat man's sweat. Walking away, my stomach is knotted with self-betrayal, but now I've got my hundred, all I have to do is find Grünwald and that feeling will soon be gone.

7

The officials say I can't go to von Weser's hospice because all three volunteer spaces have been taken and if I'd come sooner I could have gone. I'm hiding in my room. They told me to go and see Woyak, which isn't a surprise because I'm a wreck. I'm supposed to beat the shit out of Woyak for Lordowski but there's no way I can do that. I wanted to pay back the hundred to Lordowski but I don't have it: I spent it on a syringe. I know he wouldn't accept it anyway.

Breuniger said if I don't go through with the Woyak thing they'll beat me to within an inch of my life, so I'm hiding in my room but the warder's knocking and now he's standing there in the doorway. I decide to tell him.

"If I go to Woyak I've been told to attack him and if I don't I'm going to get a beating."

The warder eyes me suspiciously.

"By who?"

"You know who."

"If you attack Woyak, you'll go to a high-security institution and not get out for a very long time."

"I'm just telling you what they said to me."

"You go to Woyak and I'll tell management you're being threatened. Okay?"

"Okay."

So I'm going to Woyak's but management won't do anything.

"You look nervous Aydin," says Woyak.

"I am nervous. I'm scared."

"What are you scared of?"

"Lordowski."

"And why are you scared of Lordowski?"

"Because I'm supposed to beat you up and put you in hospital and if I don't I'm going to get hospitalised myself."

Woyak looks up from his pad and stares at me over his glasses. His pen is trembling.

"And I hope," he says in a contracted voice, fidgeting slightly in his chair, "you've decided not to beat me up?"

"Yes I have."

"I see," he says, still staring at me over his taped-up spectacles.

"And why have you decided that, Aydin?"

"Because you've done nothing wrong, what do you think? What kind of question is that?"

"Well," he says, his voice faltering, "to me that sounds like a brave decision."

"It's not brave, it's just... it's just, I can't attack someone for nothing."

"Well Aydin, perhaps that's something to be proud of. Not everyone in here can say that."

"That's why I'm scared."

Afterwards I run back to my room and hide there, but you can't lock the rooms here. Later on there is a scuffling sound at the door and someone on the other side says: "You're screwed," then there's silence except from the thumping of my heart. The whole night I wait, feeling desperate, my body shaking, which could be the fear or it could be that I need more drugs.

I'm in the corridor – the long, long corridor. I had to come out eventually: you can pee in your sink but there are things you need a toilet for, and the toilet's the place I'm most afraid of. Sure enough, Breuniger's there at the end of the corridor, posted on lookout. As I go into the toilets I hear him whistle. I try to be as quick as I can but when I come back out they're approaching down the corridor – I see their reflections in the shiny varnished stone floor, seven silhouettes, the biggest one unmistakable. I turn and walk briskly in the opposite direction, my skin prickling. Their footsteps become a clatter. "Turk, don't run away Turk, you're dead, Turk," someone calls. Ahead at the other end of the passage is a closed door.

I get that door partially open but they kick it out of my hands and I'm in a horizontal torrent of punches and kicks. I go floppy and my head hits against the door then some hands hold my arms out sideways. I've already decided not to fight, which is a first for me. The thumps and kicks don't hurt, but the sound of thumping and kicking makes me almost want to cry. Then they stop. Lordowski's holding a thick car timing chain and swinging it gently to and fro. Where did he get such a thing in here? He brings it back behind him in a slow arc, not taking his eyes off me. My head is against the door, my arms splayed, my chest heaving.

"Face or groin boys?" asks Lordowski, and they call out various parts of my body then his great limbs tauten suddenly and a growl surfaces from his oesophagus, his eyes widen and splay the way I saw them before, I sense his men moving out of the way, stretching me, he swings back the timing chain.

Then, interrupting everything, is a sharp triple-knock at the door right behind my head.

Everything goes quiet.

A faint, distinct voice comes from behind the door,

"This is Heinrich von Weser. I'm looking for an Aydin Mesüt. Is he there?"

Stone-dead silence among Lordowski's men, only my gasping breath. Lordowski's chain is back down on the shiny floor; he is listening.

Then I answer: "This is Aydin Mesüt." Immediately my arms are yanked:

"Get lost old man," booms Lordowski.

The voice behind the door replies straight away, muffled by the steel yet fully audible.

"Is that the man who admires Adolf Hitler?"

Silence. They're looking at Lordowski, saying nothing. Lordowski's chain sinks by several links further onto the floor. He is staring past me. Then he flicks his head sideways and my hands fall, my body slides down to the floor and I slump aside like an unstuffed puppet.

The faint voice speaks. "May I come in?"

Lordowski points to the door handle with his chain and one of his men opens it wide. Standing there is von Weser, alone. He steps forward right into the cluster of men, the heels of his tooled brogues clicking on the hard floor, then he sees me sitting there.

"Aydin!" – his eyes widen, his smile vanishes and he steps towards me. "Are you alright? Did I knock you over?"

"No, I fell," and I pick myself up.

Then Lordowski says: "Say what you've got to say then clear off, old man. We're busy here."

Von Weser stands up very straight again and looks up at Lordowski's great skull. Then he turns to me, his voice softening.

"Aydin, you look very pale. I'm so glad I've found you, I wanted to chat if you've got a moment."

Lordowski stirs, still holding the dangling chain. Then he speaks, but with a hint of uncertainty: "He's staying with us, old man."

Von Weser looks at Lordowski, frowns a little and closes his lips tightly. "No, he's not," he says, his voice a degree sharper now, catching off the walls and floor. I find myself thinking how well his suit fits him. A 'Visitor' tag is hanging from a lanyard around his neck.

"The thing about your idol Hitler," he says, moving slightly closer to Lordowski again and looking at his chest, "is that his manners were very coarse." Then he turns to me. "Let's go Aydin," and he makes to depart, beckoning me to go ahead of him.

But Lordowski steps in and clamps my arm in his gorilla hand.

"Get lost old man," he says.

Von Weser looks at him, then at the clamping hand, then back at him, his face unnervingly still. "I thought you wanted to help Germany?" he says abruptly, stepping right up to Lordowski's face so that he has to step back. "You are not helping Germany. But this young man wants to help me, so he is coming with me." Lordowski's eyes are moving erratically. He is looking here and there but only occasionally at von Weser. Then von

Weser moves his own hand forward in a smooth arc and takes Lordowski's wrist gently, ever so gently, like a surgeon reaching with forceps for a foreign object, looking with contempt at that object in his pincers, waiting, waiting, until slowly I feel the pressure ease, the fingers uncurl from around my arm, and then, still looking at Lordowski's hand like an item of forensic waste, von Weser releases it ever so gently, leaving it to fall away dejectedly, and repeats his beckoning gesture to me. I feel myself walking forward through the door and I hear von Weser follow then pause as he closes the door softly behind us and we head off down the corridor.

We are sitting in the director's office having my day release forms signed. I am to go with Heinrich von Weser to his hospice. Von Weser is cheerful again but the director is grumpy; he says von Weser should not have gone around the prison unaccompanied, even if he is a regular. I want to ask von Weser a barrage of questions but I also feel as happy as the sky and nothing matters. The pull of the syringe has gone right to the back of my mind, even though it's still lurking there somewhere. Everything in the office is bathed in streaming sunlight; dust particles float through the rays. I can smell the old wood of the towering, mostly empty bookcases, the leather of the director's ancient chairs and books, the acrid, sweet scent of cigars smoked alone.

The director's jowls wobble. He does not look at me, only at my papers which he thumps with a very large stamp.

"Bump! – and you're out," says von Weser, nudging me with his elbow. The director hesitates and looks up at him severely, then shakes his head and signs. "Back tonight, no later than seven."

The countryside rushes by as we drive along the old, pitted autobahn, past never-ending hectares of Brandenburg's flat grey pastureland and pine plantations dotted with flaking, mostly tumbledown buildings: a farmstead, graveyard of rusting machines; a hamlet with a church where a tiny funeral procession snakes along; a bigger village where I see a scooter tricycle driving on a cobbled street. Somebody told me one in three adults here in the East was a Stasi informer. I look at the scooter driver on his errand.

We turn off the autobahn and onto a potholed country road. I look around at von Weser. He clearly knows his way around these parts and he drives well.

"Why did you come and get me?"

He glances across at me.

"One of the other inmates didn't end up coming so I needed someone else. They said you'd been asking to come."

I say nothing.

The road has become very cratered and we've slowed right down. We arrive at a large wrought-iron double gate and a man about my age opens it for us.

"That's Jens," says von Weser. "He was in prison once too."

I look out of the back window at Jens who is closing the gates. I wonder if he got addicted like me when he was doing time. We crunch our way up a gravel drive that winds down a tunnel of trees until gardens begin to open up around us, gardens I recognise from the slide show. There are two other men quite far away, raking and bagging leaves.

"They're your co-inmates," says von Weser. "But you won't be with them, you'll be with me."

"Doing what?"

"Let's see shall we? Something's bound to come along."

We approach the manor house. Its plaster is falling away in places and it looks a bit dejected, but the roof looks newly tiled.

"Is this yours?"

"It belongs to the family, yes."

"But you're not East German are you?"

"No, but I did grow up here."

"Why did you move away?"

"The Soviets threw us out. But my old aunt stayed on, bless her."

"You have an aunt?"

"And why shouldn't I?" laughs von Weser. "Are you

implying I'm too old?"

I smile. I haven't smiled in a while. We pull up in front of the house.

"So you turned the house into a hospice?"

"That's right. I was running one in the West before, and when the Wall fell I came here to the old family home. My dear aunt! She kept hold of the old place by tooth and by nail. She feigned madness – denounced herself and her roots – because she couldn't bear to see this old place go the way of other people's houses we had known."

"What happened to them?"

"Confiscated, torn down mostly. The Soviets didn't approve of old families."

We park in front of the house and ascend stone steps that start wide and grow gradually narrower, hemmed in by two low, symmetrical, curving walls. At the top, a large wooden doorway stands open and leads into an entrance hall that rises up through all three floors of the house. Oil portraits hang all over the walls. Larger than the rest and taking centre-stage between two sweeping staircases is a portrait of Kaiser Wilhelm with a huge moustache, looking proudly out over some rural scene. He is holding a small brass telescope by his side and a dog looks up at him faithfully. His moustache makes me think of my father and uncle.

Von Weser sees me looking at the portrait.

"He knew your Emperor you know. They admired each other."

"My Emperor?"

"Abdulhamid."

"Abdulhamid? The Red Sultan?"

"Well I don't know about that," says von Weser, frowning.

"They taught us that at school," I say.

"What about your parents? What do they call him?"

"My parents? I never asked them."

"You should."

Into the entrance hall, pushed in a wheelchair by another man my age, comes the bald child from the slide show. He looks much thinner in the face; his skin is grey and dying and his eyes are sunken and purplish around the edges.

"Peter!" exclaims von Weser. "How are you?" He inclines towards the little boy with a smile and shakes his hand.

"Very well Count Heinrich," says Peter, his voice weak but spirited, a smile wrinkling his face. He looks about eleven but his face is aged. I feel suddenly ashamed of myself; a hot flush shivers over my head and torso and unexpected tears well on my eyelids. I stand behind von Weser so no one can see, but he moves away so that Peter and I are facing each other in the centre of the hall. I become aware of the hardness and beauty of the wooden floor. A hot tear rolls down my cheek and I can do nothing about it.

"Peter, this is Aydin; Aydin, Peter. Peter is the real boss around here, right Peter?" and he slaps his arm, making me flinch. He looks so delicate.

Peter smiles at me and holds out a grey, spindly hand that pokes out from inside his oversize tunic.

"Pleased to meet you."

I have to step right forward to take his hand; I have never touched such a thin, ill-looking limb but it grips mine quite strongly and I shake it, then I wipe my nose.

"Sorry," I say. "Pleased to meet you."

"Why don't you take Peter for a stroll around the garden?" says von Weser, and he nods to the carer, who moves away from behind the wheelchair.

"Alright," I say. "Let's go," and I go around and grasp the still-warm wheelchair handles. From here I can look right onto the top of Peter's head. It is not entirely bald: there are isolated strands of very thin grey hair sprouting out of it, like photos of atomic devastation which I try to push out of my mind. Peter leans his head right back and looks up at me for a second, then looks ahead again.

"We should go out by the side door," he says, "but if you're strong enough you can wheel me down the steps, even though you're not supposed to." Peter looks ahead and waits, his thin little hands resting on the armrests. I move forward out of the front door, the lush gardens flowing away on all sides. Rivers of velvet lawn wend between islands of shrubs and flowers of pink, purple, red and yellow, and further away trees bend their great heads to a breeze. Insects skim. The steps are quite steep and as I approach them and tilt back the chair I see Peter's ears move: he's smiling. As I clunk down each step as carefully as I can, his little body bounces inside the ill-fitting tunic.

At the bottom of the steps we turn right and go along the front of the house.

"Are you from the prison?" he asks.

"Yes. I'm out for the day."

"What did you do?"

"I drove for some drug dealers."

He is silent for a few moments.

"Cool."

"It's not cool," I say.

"Oh," he says, still looking straight ahead.

"And what about you," I ask. "Why are you here?"

"I'm going to die. That's what they say. But... you never know."

A butterfly wobbles across our path. The sun is warm. I wipe my eyes and nose with my sleeve, trying not to let him notice.

"It's okay if you cry," he says after a while. "I do."

I've got to stop for a second and turn away. I feel the urge welling up to cry properly, to shout even – not just about him, about everything – but then I think he won't like that so I pull it in. I blow my nose one nostril at a time into a flowerbed.

"So if you're not going to die," I ask, "what's your plan?"

"My plan is to ask God so many times to live that he has to say yes."

"Aha," I say.

"My parents don't like me saying things like that. Do you believe in God?"

I don't answer because I don't know the answer. The answer is stuck.

Peter tilts his head right back again and looks up at me, then looks ahead again. I push him far into the gardens. He observes everything intensely. A bee goes by, he looks at it, so I look at it too. We pass two other wheelchair-bound patients with their carers and Peter greets them, so I do too. The sun is warming my shoulders and I can smell grass cuttings, oak leaves and dandelions whose scent rises from the lawns. Peter seems to love everything he sees.

I take Peter along a path and through a gate where we're not really supposed to go. I want to keep him as long as I can. I wish I could stay here with him.

"But what if you do die, Peter?"

"We all die some time."

He's not exactly chirpy but he's not gloomy either. He's settled between the two.

"Aren't you afraid that God won't listen when you ask?"

"What?" He looks up at me again. "Why would you think that?"

Later, back at the house, I'm washing up in the kitchen, immersing my hands in warm water and handling the bowls and spoons. Then someone comes hurrying in, a short, thin, upright man with high cheekbones, close-cropped hair and oriental eyes, dressed in a black jacket and tie and carrying a navy blue blazer across his arm.

"Herr Aydin?" He says. "Could you put this on? Mr von Weser would like you to join him for lunch."

I dry my hands and leave the kitchen together with this man, pulling on the blazer as I go. It smells of old scent and it fits.

I'm ushered straight into the dining room. Its walls are burgundy; there is an elaborate black marble fireplace on the left; on the opposite side, large windows. The head of a wild boar is mounted on the wall above the fireplace, staring out through glazed eyes. There are other stuffed animals mounted around the room including a stag's head and a large, leathery, bored-looking pike in a glass display case.

The table is polished dark mahogany with three huge candle-holders on it. Heinrich von Weser is sitting at the far end with four others, two along each side. He stands as I enter and gestures to the empty seat on his right. I slip into place.

"This is Aydin Mesüt who has joined us for the day," he says. They nod and smile at me. Sitting opposite are a middle-aged man and woman. "Aydin, this is Mr and Mrs Noske from the nearby village, and this,"

151

he says, holding out his palm towards the two men on my right, is my great-nephew Andreas and his friend from England, Simon."

I look around at them and they smile at me.

"Welcome, Aydin," says Andreas. His voice is deep and strong, his hair blond, wavy and mid-length and he looks about twenty-five. Simon is a similar age and although his features are very different he has the same air of assurance about him; he greets me in good German but with an English accent. Both are wearing sharply pressed shirts.

"Simon is here helping with our Foundation," says von Weser. "Andreas helps run our business interests."

"What business are you in?" I ask.

"Forests mainly," replies Andreas. "I don't know whether you'd call it business really," and he laughs apologetically. "It's usually just keeping the banks at bay."

The small man with high cheek-bones enters silently through a side door carrying three plates and places them in front of von Weser, myself and Mr Noske. In the middle of each are asparagus spears dripping with melted butter. My mouth waters. This is the opposite of the prison. The butler brings in three more plates and sets them before the others.

"Straight from the garden," says von Weser as he starts.

Everyone begins to eat. I'm glad for the wall-hanging animals because they give me something to look at.

Von Weser notices me looking at them. "Some of my former friends," he says, nodding up towards the staring animals' heads. "That one there," he continues, "the little deer next to the stag, was actually a family pet when I lived here as a boy. When it died we had it mounted. Aunt Carla had them all locked up in the cellars for forty-five years, which is why they look so shabby. How is she by the way?"

"She's well, uncle," replies Andreas.

"Good. Perhaps you could take Aydin up to meet her after lunch?"

The asparagus is soft and tastes of subtle things I don't know. The butter on it is very salty. I think of my mother's food and the warmth of our flat, and the way she too makes proper meals that we ate together at a table like this, only smaller.

The butler comes and places some casseroles and platters on a sideboard next to the fireplace. Once we've finished the asparagus he takes away our little plates. I am wondering why I am here and keep expecting to be told, but nothing is said. Von Weser doesn't mention to anybody where I have come from. Andreas and Simon lead the way in helping themselves at the sideboard. There is mashed potato, some roasted pieces of small bird, a ragout and green beans. I serve myself the way I see them serving. My hands are shaking again and I feel slightly feverish. I try to hide it.

After the meal is over, Andreas takes me up a sweeping staircase and along to the end of a carpeted corridor where he tells me to wait. He knocks at a door and enters a dimmed room without awaiting a reply, closing the door behind him. After a minute the door opens again.

"Come in. Aunt Carla is ready to see you."

I step inside.

"Who's that, who's that?" The voice is loud and melodic like some great jungle bird. I cannot see its owner. Thin shafts of sunlight bear down at forty-five degrees between tall, thick, velvet curtains like a theatre's.

"It's Aydin, Aunt Carla, Aydin," shouts Andreas.

"Aydin? Who's Aydin?"

"I just told you, Aunt Carla," shouts Andreas, smiling.

"Oh yes, yes, don't go telling me everything twice. Come forward young man, let me see you."

I still cannot see her; my eyes are adjusting to the darkness. I step forward, dizzy from the museum air and feeling slightly sick. Then I begin to make her out, enveloped in garments that flow down into the pool of an ornamental carpet. There she is: her face deeply wrinkled, flaps of skin hanging in loops down her neck, her head quite still, a pronounced nose, her large eyes watery and all-seeing. Despite her age she is quite beautiful.

"Come forward young man, don't be so hesitant for

goodness sake. I can't see you. Aha! From Turkey yes?"

"Yes."

Then I ask Andreas in a whisper: "What should I call her?"

"I'm not deaf!" she retorts. "Call me Carla if you like. That's the done thing now," she says rather sourly.

"What would you prefer?"

"What? Oh no, I don't have a title, don't believe in them. Responsible for so much mess. So much mess," and she lifts a hand in a gesture, then sinks it again onto the arm of her velvet high-back chair. "Sit, sit! Why are you standing there like that?"

Andreas reverses apologetically out of the room. The old lady pulls herself slowly forward, her chair creaking, and peers closely at me, grasping both its arms for stability.

"Hmm. Did Heinrich bring you here? Are you here doing community service?"

"Not exactly," I say. "Sorry, but… I don't feel comfortable calling you by your first name."

"Well," she replies, glancing behind me to check that Andreas has gone then lowers her voice, "you can call me countess. But don't tell them, they might take back the house," and just for a moment she grins mischievously.

"I heard someone call Mr von Weser 'count'."

"Huh," she says, and waves her hand. "And so they should. He's done so much for them, the ingrates. Are you helping with the hospice?"

"Yes, but just for the day."

"Just for the day? Hmm, I suppose that's long enough to be with all those dying people though. Terribly gloomy! You won't catch me down there with all those invalids." She chuckles to herself.

"Actually, I kind of like it. I met a young boy downstairs who's dying, but he's got spirit."

"Spirit?" She frowns as if she has not understood me. "Yes I suppose he must have, poor thing. It's all the morose ones I can't stand," and she shifts in her chair, making her clothes rustle. "We're all dying, sooner or later. When your time comes, it comes." Her posture and gestures are peacock-like.

What she says seems a bit unfair on the people downstairs and I feel like changing the subject.

"Count von Weser says he knew Hitler. Did you know him?"

The countess pulls in the blanket on her knee and looks horrified, then she snaps at me:

"Don't mention that horrible little man to me!" She lifts herself up in her chair and looks at me through steely eyes. Then she sinks a little. "But did Heinrich tell you he tried to kill Hitler? Far too modest," and she tuts.

"He mentioned it, but not really."

"Far too modest. Many of us were involved. Heinrich played a major role, even though he was young. He was attached to Rommel, and Rommel was very involved. Ah! What a man Rommel was."

"Count von Weser was with Rommel?"

Even I know Rommel.

"Yes. He was there when Rommel was executed."

"I thought he committed suicide?"

"No, no, he was forced to take cyanide, otherwise they would have executed him and imprisoned his family. As it was, they let them be and Hitler sent flowers to his funeral. His son's the mayor of Stuttgart now."

"He told me you stayed here when the Soviets came."

At this the countess turns away and her eyes suddenly seem to be looking at something very far away. She says nothing. I cough.

"You stayed here all the…"

"No no…" she interjects, waving a hand at me but still looking away. There is a long silence and I hear my heart pounding.

"They did things," she says finally.

I blush and she glances at me.

"Don't worry," she says, "you weren't to know. I wasn't the only one though. No no! They went into every house, I can tell you, even into the schools. But that was a long time ago. After that they left us alone, they installed a government to do their bidding. It was another madness to replace the one before."

"I'm sorry."

She straightens herself. Her head is quite erect. "Enough about me. What about you? You didn't answer my question."

"What question?"

"Are you doing community service?"

"No. I'm from the prison."

"The prison?" She screws her face up and turns down her mouth, looking at me uncomprehendingly. "Whatever were you doing there? – no! Never mind. I don't want to know. Heinrich brought you here did he? Well. You've disgraced yourself, I'm sure. Correct whatever you've done young man, as soon as you can."

She pauses.

"And what part of Turkey does your family come from?"

"I don't know."

"What?" she says, looking astonished. "Why ever not?"

"My parents never talk about it, or about their parents. We're not allowed to."

"Well," she says, staring at me. "That's unusual, but they must have their reasons."

She extends her neck and peers at me even more closely.

"Are you married?"

"No."

"You Turks still marry don't you?"

"Yes, of course, it's just... I haven't met the right person."

"The right person? The right person?" she says imperiously. "That's not the way the world works young man."

That's the kind of thing my parents would say, but it feels different. There's a knock at the door and it opens. I turn to see von Weser enter.

"Good afternoon Aunt Carla," he says loudly, and goes to kiss her cheek. Have you been telling Aydin about the house?"

"No, I've been telling him about you," she says, holding onto his hand a little as he reverses to sit in another chair.

"Oh dear," says von Weser, "not much to talk about then," and he winks at me in the gloom.

"And I was telling him," interrupts the countess in an imposing tone, "that there's no such thing as finding 'the right person' – but he didn't believe a word I was saying, just as nobody else does."

"Oh," says von Weser, smiling, "don't listen to her, Aydin."

"What?" says the countess, looking back at von Weser, "You've joined the rest of them? Huh!" We all laugh; I feel relieved by his presence.

"Aunt Carla, I'm going to take Aydin now if you don't mind. We've got more work to do before the day's out."

"Of course," says the countess, settling back into erectness and smiling. "It's been a pleasure to meet you, young man. You've got fighting spirit, I can see – like Heinrich here. It was fighting in a good cause that earned our ancestors all this in the first place," and she gestures to the surroundings – "when fighting was still something to be proud of. So fight on, Aydin! But going around in prisons? She grimaces. That's not who you are. You can't go about not being who you are."

We stand and say goodbye to her and go back into the bright corridor. I had forgotten about the outside world, the beauty of the house, the warmth of the day, the day which will soon be over and the prison and drugs that I'll soon be going back to.

"We've still got an hour before I have to take you back," says von Weser, reading my thoughts. "Want to go to the kitchen or out into the garden?"

"The garden," I reply.

"Thought so."

I am weeding a flowerbed, crouching on my haunches. I have an hour to go but I wish I could stay here with these people, where maybe things could get better. Lordowski is back at the prison but it's not him I'm afraid of – it's the boredom, and behind the boredom the needle. I'm afraid of the needle and the pills. I'm afraid of hating myself. I pull out one tiny weed after the next, shaking off the black soil, wondering what to do. A discovered worm makes its escape, burrowing between the tiny boulders of earth. The worm is halfway gone. I lift up a soil-boulder to make it easier for him.

What the countess said makes me think about my family. I know my grandparents died; that's all I've been told. And that they were fighters, whatever that means. A wheelchair goes by pushed by a young man who I can tell is not from prison but who is not dressed as a nurse. Maybe he's doing community service instead of going to the army. Lots of people from Berlin do that.

In the car on the way back to the prison I want to ask von Weser to intervene with Lordowski or do something else to help me, but when the time comes and we're driving along, it doesn't feel right to ask.

When I think of Lordowski, I'm not actually afraid of him. And when the prison gates finally appear and we drive through, I do feel afraid of the drugs, but I feel something unexpected mixed in: hope.

8

From now on I am going to do things right. I got up this morning and washed for the prayer, which, in the dirty world I've created for myself, made me feel like some kind of outlaw. And when I did the prayer, I felt like I was disobeying my own urges, which felt even better. The shivers and shakes are still there, but this is going to be how I make a new beginning. Plus, I'm going to try to go back to the hospice. The people there are cleaner than here, safer than here, better than here, better even than the world I know back home – except maybe Uncle Mejid. He's got the same self-assurance as von Weser and Countess Carla. My parents were like that once, but only when I was younger.

Breakfast is coming and I'll see Lordowski and I'm

going to go up and talk to him – make peace, something, come what may. What matters is that I do something.

Breakfast time. I'm coming into the canteen, scanning the tables for his profile, my heart battering my
ribs.

Sliding up at my shoulder comes Marlowe Grünwald. He holds my arm to stop me.

"Here," he says, placing something into my hand.

"I've gotten supply again. You're a good boy."

He moves away smoothly.

I feel two tiny items in my sweaty palm. I stride
angrily over to the bin and hold my hand over it.

But there could be utility in these items. I could sell
them and pay off Lordowski. If I get beaten up like
they promised, they may be painkillers. I can always
decide when the time comes. If I'm going to be strong
enough to keep off drugs, then maybe having some
with me and not taking them will help me be strong. I
pocket them.

Lordowski is not here in the canteen; no one knows
where he is. At work I am joined by Kleemann again,
not Breuniger. Maybe management has intervened
with Lordowski and his men after all.

"Jörg, I'm sorry I stole from you. I'll pay you back."

"How was your 'work experience'?" he says sarcastically, not looking at me. "Bet you liked it out there."

"So what?"

Jörg Kleemann is silent and we get on with sorting

electrical components and ignoring each other.

Over the next few days I see Lordowski's men but not Lordowski. They're nothing without him, don't even look me in the eye.

I am lying on my bed wondering whether to go on doing the prayers. It seems like a good idea but then again it may not be the only way. My father says you have to do them, but one of my friends said if you don't, once you fast for Ramadan your slate is wiped clean. But what if you die beforehand? I think of Peter and his dying. I have the two pills in my hand and am toying with them, then suddenly, just to spite my better self and before I can think properly, I put them both in my mouth and swallow one but spit the other one out, jolting upright, shocked at myself, sickened, then I pick the spat-out one up and put it behind my television set. I wonder whether to try to vomit the other one out and I go to the sink to try but I can't; maybe I can wash for the prayer after all. Maybe it's pointless now.

All at once the swimming feeling washes over me but it's not the same this time. I go to my door and back to the television, then sit on the edge of my bed and rock backward and forward, holding my head, trying to cry out and shake it off but it's coming over like a great wave. The best thing is to eat the other pill now so it can join the other one, or once this one's worn off so I just have one long trip and then call it a day and to hell with Marlowe Grünwald and the rest of them.

How could I have been so weak as to accept this from him? I feel afraid. I fall over sideways onto my bed and stare at the wall which flows. I imagine myself in the bottom of a pit with just a small circle of sky showing high up above and I am never going to get out and see the sky again. Then I drop off to sleep and dream of being in a freezer and then in the Arctic or Antarctic, then von Weser is there trudging across the snow but he cannot hear me and disappears into the blizzard. Then Yez the Kurd appears and it's me throwing his cat out of the window this time, not Zola; he leans out of the window to catch it and I push him out after it, then he's hanging on the sill by his fingers, four floors up from the concrete yard, his anguished, begging eyes looking up at me.

I wake up in a shivering sweat with my covers off and it's night already and the lights are out and I desperately need the toilet but I can't get up, something is holding me down. Struggling back to my senses, I find the other pill and play with it in my hands. My head is pulsing dully. Then I put the pill in my mouth and swallow so it can join its friend.

It is breakfast. I cannot find Marlowe Grünwald anywhere and I don't want food, I just want to finish off this experience one final time to get this thing out of my system. Maybe he has something much stronger so that I can say I've tried everything and there's nothing more to try, and maybe that will block the terror that's coming at me from somewhere. I hang around the canteen and some inmates push past me and say something I can't hear.

At work I rock back and forth on my chair. They're paying us tomorrow; I just have to hold out until then. Back in my room in the afternoon I lie down and hold myself, rocking. I cannot think. I'm way beyond praying now.

The next day I get my pay and, sure enough, Grünwald is in the canteen at supper.

"You got anything strong?"

"What like, really strong?"

"Yeah."

He looks at me suspiciously then delves into the pocket of his white catering coat.

"Here. Two hundred. Don't tell anyone. And don't come to me if it's too strong."

"I don't have two hundred. I only have fifty."

"Show me your fifty."

I show him the creased note.

"Okay," he says, looking around, "just this once, no more loans after this, and you pay me the rest by Monday, alright?"

"Alright."

I take the object wrapped in tissue and go straight to my room. There are voices inside saying stop but I push them away. I am shaking. I unwrap it. The liquid in the syringe is completely clear; I push the plunger a little and some gleaming drops run down the steel needle. This is the last one ever. It'll be the ultimate. After this I won't do any more.

I apply the needle to my scabby vein, press it a little, denting the skin but not piercing, then I insert it slowly into the skin and watch it creep up inside the vein, pushing a bruised hump along, curious. Still I do not press the plunger. The neon light in my room buzzes and a fly goes about its business.

I envisage Peter coming at me in his wheelchair. He looks angry, he is approaching me, his gaunt, purple features smeared with salty messy tears. He comes right up to me, his eyes accusing. I hold out my hand to him but he is turning around and leaving me, wheeling away through the garden, butterflies and birds going with him. Gone. I search for another face. I see my uncle and he looks at me, the first time I have ever seen him terrified, a man normally free of fear. Then I imagine Imam Osman and he is smiling down malevolently from his pulpit. It jolts me and I put his image aside. I try to imagine the Master but I cannot recall his face, only the back of his head and his pigtail. Then I think of Steffi and in my mind, all she wants is sex, sex, sex – except even that's a lie we've agreed on. Then, although I did not want to, I think of Heinrich von Weser and he looks away in displeasure.

With a shout I tear the needle out of my arm. Shouting again I hurl it with all my might against the wall. The needle detaches, the syringe comes to a rest, its frothed fluid contents settling. I pick it up and, seized by anger, lift the end of my bed, put the syringe beneath its metal foot then stamp hard on the bed-frame, shouting. The syringe splits, casting liquid in a star. Someone thumps on the wall and shouts. I look at the tentacles of liquid, take my towel, mop them up, take the towel to the sink and unleash the tap on it, splashing water everywhere. I lie on my bed and shout, thumping the mattress and pillow as hard as I can until, exhausted and panting, I slump down into the mattress, cry angry tears and shout with rage.

I wake later that night. All is dark, all is quiet. I am alone and the pills have completely worn off. I feel sober – shaking still, but sober – and I hear my heart beating steadily. I am cornered. I cannot go out, cannot stay still, can't even cry, though I want to. Then I am on a riverbank. On the other side of the river a man is beckoning to me. He is kind and could be young or old. I want to go to him. He speaks:

"Ask."

I try to speak back but no words come.

"Ask," he repeats. "Ask."

I awaken again and all is still quiet and dark. I pull myself from my bed, shivering and shaking, take a change of fresh clothes out of my tiny drawer, open my door and look along the corridor towards the bathroom and the showers, then tiptoe out on bare feet. I shower and change then decide to wash for the prayer just as another act of defiance, an affront to my own weakness. And because I now have nothing left to lose. Back in my room I take a clean, threadbare towel and spread it in the space in the corner. I don't know what good this is going to do. I stand there and begin, reciting what little I know, then I bow, then stand, then prostrate my head onto the towel and stay there for some time, feeling the coolness of the night air at floor level. While I am there I say inside myself: "Thank you." Thank you for this little space. Then I come up again and I repeat it all again, saying the same thing, only several times for good measure. Then I sit and finish off. Now I just stay there and everything is completely still, even the inside of me. My hands are shaking but they feel peripheral, like something detached from myself. I smell the cleanliness of my clothes, feel the thin towel beneath me, protecting me a little from the hardness of the floor. Then I stand and, because the night is so peaceful, I do the whole thing over again and I ask. I ask to go clean and for the other things I want.

9

Adelbert Woyak's glasses are more askew than usual and the tape is coming unravelled; I feel like telling him they look wrong, but I'm wary of how he might take it. He sighs and reviews the notes on his pad, then looks up at me, one eye magnified like a fish in a bowl.

"How are you Aydin?"

"I'm alright."

"I see you're half way through your time here if all goes well?"

"Yep."

He shifts in his seat and picks up his pencil.

"Are you sleeping well?"

"Yes, I am now."

"Were you not before?"

"No."

"Why do you think that might be?"

"Because I know what to do."

"Really?" he says, putting down his pencil and looking up through the squint frames. "That sounds positive. Would you like to share it?"

"I want to go and help at the hospice."

He looks at me. "That's commendable. What attracts you to that?"

"I dunno. I just feel at home there, I feel I can help people."

"That I can understand."

I don't really like his answering like that, always accepting everything. It makes me feel combative.

"Is that why you do this work, Mr Woyak?" I ask.

His one eye looks bulbous, the other is obscured by the frame as he stares at me. I wish he would straighten his glasses.

"Yes," he says falteringly, "I mean, that's part of it."

"What's the other part?"

"Well," he says, twiddling his pencil, "I find it interesting, the way people work."

I don't like him enjoying the way I work, but I say nothing. Then I say:

"There's this boy at the hospice called Peter. He's eleven and he's dying of leukaemia but he's – he's just so positive. He loves everything he sees."

"Go on," replies Woyak, and he leans forwards and taps his pencil against his lip, looking at me intently.

"I think about him every day. I want to be like him,

but without dying."

"Yes," he says. "And how might you try to be like him?"

"I dunno," I reply. "I just want to see him again, maybe look after him. Maybe he'll get better."

I suddenly feel I shouldn't say anything more to him. He waits for a while. "So," he says eventually, "the hospice, then? Good old Mr von Weser." He makes a note.

"Are you experiencing any other problems you would like to tell me about?"

"No."

"No threats?"

"No."

"Drugs?"

"No," I say, which is untrue; I'm feeling urges all the time, shooting through my nerves, but I won't tell him.

Woyak looks at me for a few seconds more, then writes something else in his pad.

"Well," he continues, "that's all for now then. But I hope you'll let me know if you want to speak about anything else."

Autumn is coming. I've got a new workmate called Selim. He's Turkish and used to do martial arts so we have something to talk about. We talk about training, how hard it is, and about the few fights we've had;

we talk about starting to train here in prison, maybe even teaching some inmates. We talk about girls and about what we're going to do when we get out. He was caught shoplifting a few times. He's not in for long.

Some weeks later he arrives at work high: he thinks I can't tell but his eyes look unseeingly at me and he's making an effort to act normally. I'm upset with him.

At breakfast the day after, I watch him enter the canteen. He is my height but a lot broader. Not like the bodybuilders, though; his bulkiness is softer and he carries it easier. He has a crew cut. His face is round and pale, his blue-green eyes big and innocent like a child's.

He bumps into Grünwald and they exchange words; Grünwald hands him something.

I get up, tipping my chair over and knocking the table so that people's drinks slosh and I march over to Grünwald: the whole room goes quiet to watch what I'm going to do.

"Hey snake, leave him alone," I shout at Grünwald.

"It's okay Aydin," says Selim in Turkish, moving between us. "It's fine. It's nothing," and he laughs, patting my arm with a forced smile, trying to make a joke of it.

"No it's not Selim," I say in German.

Everyone's watching, including two warders. People here love trouble.

"He's getting you hooked. It'll mess you up."

The warders approach.

"Sit down Mesüt," says the tall warder, swinging his

baton casually.

"What?" I reply, "he's selling drugs and you're protecting him?"

"Selling drugs?" says Grünwald sarcastically. "You wish. Search me then! Search me!" and he holds out his arms to the warders and grins, showing rotten teeth.

"Calm down Mesüt, you're imagining things," says the shorter warder, ushering me away from Grünwald. I look at Selim for support but he moves to the food queue and turns his back on me.

Later at work, Selim's not there. I feel sick and there's a ticking noise in my head. When a warder comes by I demand to see the director and in the afternoon I'm called to his office.

The director is more puffed up now that von Weser's not here. He takes a short, thick cigar from a wooden box on his desk, clips the end and sucks a flame in through crackling leaves.

"So," he says slowly from behind a cloud of smoke, "You want to speak to me about drug dealing?"

"Yes," I reply. "It's Grünwald. He's selling them and even giving them away."

The director gazes at me dourly. His lower eyelids hang down like a bloodhound's, revealing the wet red inner-lids below his bloodshot whites. Plumes of smoke eddy outwards from his jowly face.

"You know," he says, leaning back into his leather

chair and pausing to tug on the cigar again, "I run the cleanest, safest institution in Brandenburg and I'm proud of it. How do I do it?" He looks out of the window at some distant inmates strolling and sends some smoke in their direction. "I do it by minimising problems and controlling sources. You understand? Minimising problems – and controlling sources."

"Sources? You mean Grünwald? He's giving drugs away to get people hooked! I got hooked!"

The director leans forward; his chair groans. He fixes his bloodhound eyes on me, staring long and hard.

"Young man, Grünwald is a model prisoner. He's never in all his time stepped out of line. If you have anything to report you may do so in writing. But I warn you that should you even suggest you have been taking drugs here, then the deal which we were about to offer you will be withdrawn and you will be moved somewhere much less agreeable than my little stable."

I stare at him and swallow a painful lump, hiding my shaking hands beneath the table.

"What deal?"

The director looks at me long and slow.

"It will be explained to you tomorrow, and the papers will be ready to sign. But as you're here, I'll give you a preview, then you can go away and think about it."

The ash on his cigar is growing quite long, but he doesn't seem to notice.

"We know you were running drugs for Zola Malodich and collecting debts for Benjamin Lok. We know Lok's a violent criminal and Zola supplies drugs around Berlin. But our problem is," he says, "nobody wants to speak. Everyone's scared. They're loyal to them like you were at your trial."

"I don't know anything about what Zola Malodich and Benjamin Lok do."

"Ah, well if that's your attitude," says the director, raising his eyebrows and sitting back in his chair, "you can sit here and do your time while Malodich and Lok live in freedom. It's your choice. But if you testify, you can go home and they will come and take your place – except not here. Somewhere for really bad people, somewhere much worse. And for much longer, so they won't be bothering you again."

"What about when they eventually get out?"

"You'll be offered protection."

I look out across the yard. The strolling inmates have gone. I can't get the thought of the pills out of my head.

His tone softens. "Surely you're better than this, Mesüt," he says, leaning forward until he is almost too close, looking right at me. "Squandering yourself in prison." His eyes are cold and watery. "Zola Malodich and Benjamin Lok are the real bad people, not you. You can trade places and do the world a favour. It's up to you."

He watches for my reaction. Then without taking his eyes off me, he moves his cigar deftly over an ashtray at the moment a long chunk of ash drops off. The whole room is full of smoke.

"Alright, let me think about it," I say eventually. He keeps staring at me, waiting. Then I add: "I'll tell you tomorrow."

"Good," says the director, leaning back and smiling. "You're dismissed."

I get up and leave.

I'm lying in my cell in a cold sweat, turning it over and over in my mind. What if I agree and tell the director about Zola and the Master? They'll want revenge, but I'll be free to start anew. I imagine a tidy, clean life, maybe out in West Germany in some sleepy town amid woodlands and squirrels; or living in Hamburg, anonymously, successfully, among fashionably dressed people who know what they're doing. I went to Hamburg once: honking container ships sail out from the docks to the big wide world. Maybe I'll board one of those to Turkey, where I'll disappear into Istanbul's spicy, smoggy sprawl. The Turks claim it's the biggest city in the world. Zola wouldn't find me there. I even speak the language, so I could be a native. Not that I've ever been; I don't even know what it's really like. I might have distant cousins there, working among the bins and shops and offices.

Or I could go and work for von Weser at the hospice, which is what I really want. But one day Zola and the Master will get out and they'll come and find me.

Or I could just stay quiet and do my time, then I won't have to worry about Zola or the Master.

They tell me Lordowski's back in prison and looking for me. They say he wants to finish my punishment. I wonder how quickly the deal would get me out of here if I sign?

Next day, Selim comes to the worktable, apologises about the Grünwald incident and thanks me for speaking up for him. I can tell he's high.

"No worries Selim. I got hooked on Grünwald's pills myself and now I'm trying to stay off drugs but it's hard. I think about them every day."

"Yeah," he replies, leaning back in his chair and staring through his electricals tray. He's only half listening, but I keep talking, half to myself.

"I went to the director yesterday to tell on Grünwald, but he said they're going to offer me a deal. I have to tell them about some people I know who run drugs in Berlin, then they'll let me just walk out of here."

Selim glances at me then goes back to rummaging through his tray. I watch him, twiddling a cable and looking closely at its plug, examining it from every side. It's as if he's not hearing me at all, but he must be. Something in my stomach starts to sink.

The director doesn't call me. Two days later, Lordowski appears at breakfast, surrounded by his men and they're staring at me. I take my tray and sit alone but they all come up, pull chairs around me and sit.

I look down at my roll and cheese. I can't eat being watched.

"You escaped the last beating, Turk," says Lordowski quietly. "But not this one. We've got a message from Zola and your karate master. We'll deliver it outside."

He scrapes back his chair and shoves the table so my juice tips over, spilling an orange patch between the plate, knife and paper napkin. The others stand up after him and one of them punches my head as he leaves. I glance at the guards; they look away quickly.

I stare at my lonely white roll. My heart is jumping at my ribs and I feel like peeing my pants with fear and anger. But I'm not going to. I'm not going to cave in at all this time.

I shove my breakfast tray away and send my chair toppling back. Lordowski's men disappear through the washing-up entrance and I follow them, striding.

Someone grasps my arm: Selim.

"No Aydin, no," he hisses. "No."

His hand is shaking violently and his eyes are full of fear.

"Sorry Aydin," he stumbles on. Sorry, I... I just..."

"Let go Selim. Come and watch. I thought you liked fighting?" I shake his hand off my arm and go after Lordowski.

Lordowski's back is much bigger than anyone else's. My fear has gone. I always wanted to fight someone really big.

"Lordowski," I say, turning his head and stopping the whole posse in its tracks. "What's the message from Zola and the Master?"

"Oh, looky here!" he says to his men. They shift nervously, gawping at me.

"The Turk wants his message," mocks Lordowski in his booming voice. "Come on then. It's waiting for you through here in the laundry room, Turk. After you." He gestures through an open door to where the big machines work day and night.

I hurry through to evade anything they might try to do from behind. I want to fight him front-on. I don't care about the outcome.

They file in almost obediently after me. The machines are tumbling, some are spinning. It's humid and smells of chemicals. An inmate is forking a load of washing out of a trolley. When he sees me and Lordowski and the group of men, he drops the load and goes quickly away. Some machines stop, some rumble on. Water hisses into them, suds splash against the thick glass portholes.

I face the gang. Lordowski comes straight at me. I knot my fists into rocks like the Master taught me. I take my stance like the Master taught me.

Lordowski's whole gorilla frame comes around me, all over me. He tries to grab me but I get away, dodging down and back. I can smell his breath. His green eyes have gone the monster way they were when he punched skin off that man's skull. One of his huge fists clips the tip of my nose as I move further back and away. Shouting, he sprays me with spit.

A machine at my back begins to accelerate into a frantic spin. I think of the tournament when I was losing because I did nothing. In the dojo, the Master used to drill me by myself, getting me to side kick a pad again and again and again because I could knock him back with more force than anyone.

Then I crash into a metal table and duck another fist, but as I try to escape, something comes down on the back of my head and smashes me against thin stainless steel. I feel nothing; I only hear the clanging sound. Lordowski roars but I'm not afraid of him. All I'm afraid of is giving up like last time.

I see the Master's face, angry at us for our floppy kicks. Then in my mind I hear the war cry. I stand and face Lordowski and knot my fists again. His men are rooted to their places; some of them shout words of anxious encouragement. For a moment I think they're shouting for me. Machines are spinning and thudding furiously.

I'm probably only going to get one chance at this. I shout the war cry at the top of my voice, shaking every particle in the room with sound. I scream it.

Lordowski falters and his eyebrows crunch up in the middle. I step forward quickly, turning on the ball of my front foot so its heel points at him, then I shoot my other leg forward with my whole self behind it, screaming the war cry again, electrocuting every nerve in me.

My right heel connects into his middle so perfectly, splitting the bands of meat, knocking out the air and the phlegm. He folds up and staggers back, buckling, coughing, collapsing onto the floor.

Then I hear confusion behind me like hyenas gone mad, crashing things out of the way to come at me. Blows rain down on my back, my head, my legs, sending me crashing into the buckled form of Lordowski. My face hits his knee as I fall to the ground.

Then the pain starts on all sides.

They get busy all over me, cursing and shouting.

Something is placed on my kidney area and someone stamps on it.

A metal boot cap hits my head, making the world sing and stars fly in a green spangled heaven. The sounds don't stop; the hitting, the shouting, the kicks. Someone stamps on my foot and I hear a crack.

Another foot is on my neck, then it presses down and it becomes hard to breath. My mouth tastes of hot, sweet salt. Then there is a voice from the floor near me: Lordowski's.

"Zola says, don't you dare take the deal," he rasps, spitting fluids, fighting for his breath. "But I'm not giving you the fuckin' chance."

Then someone's boot goes into my head and I go far away to another world.

10

There is the peep, peep, peep of my heart. I see nothing because my eyes are glued shut with gum. I do not feel my body at all. I hear blood coursing gently through my ears.

I remember everything. The fight. Kicking Lordowski. The attack that followed. The crushed ankle. The head kicks. The kidney. The broken windpipe. The message from Zola not to take the deal.

I remember the world I went to after that. There were seagulls there but the sky was dark and there was no sea, and there was the clicking of castanets but no Spain and no dancers; there were conger eels in submarine cliffs. There was seaweed and mountains and grass savannahs.

Then, there was something hard to think about,

not because it was so bad, because it was so good. It was the end of shadows. The shadows were doubts. It was the end of tiredness. The tiredness was me. I was there, but I was there without the heavy weight of me.

The fight had been good, just like I wanted it to be. It was my best ever fight, even though I lost, because I got in my best kick and put him down and he needed his scum friends to rescue him. My mind is light and carefree. I cannot feel my body, but I am starting to feel my head now. A pumping ache, tracking my beating heart. The ache spreads slowly.

The ache grows. A tiny gap has opened in my eyegum, a slit into pain. A white ceiling with lights – hospital. But I knew that already because I smelled it.

I think of my father and mother. Maybe they have been here. Something is stopping me from moving my head: some blocks like polystyrene press tightly against my temples. I wiggle my fingers. They work. And my toes – but only the left ones work. The right ones make a sharp pain in the ankle, but at least I can feel pain there, which means it has not been removed – unless it's a phantom pain.

Then I think of Steffi. I miss her and want to cry, but I can't.

Someone is present in the room.

"Aydin?" says the voice of a man I don't know. "Aydin? Can you hear me?"

I swallow, which hurts like mad, then I open my mouth to speak but only a hoarse rasp comes out, and that hurts too. The pain in my head is spreading down my neck.

"Don't try to speak if it's too difficult," says the voice. Then it speaks to someone else. "He's out of the coma. Tell Meyerling."

Then a woman's voice speaks to me. "You're in hospital Aydin. You were assaulted in prison. There's a lot of damage."

I know those things. I close my gum-eye slit and sleep immediately.

I cannot move. I locate myself by the places of pain: the windpipe shows me where my neck is; the throbbing ankle marks my lower-right extremity. The pulsating kidney marks the side of the small of my back. Today, or this night – there are no days or nights here – the beeping stopped because they pulled off the sticky probes listening to my heart. The silence is better. My parents came again a while ago, but I pretended to sleep. They talked together. They sounded calm, which made me glad. Then they left.

Doctor Meyerling says I have a ruptured kidney, a crushed ankle, a broken vertebra, a fractured skull and bleeding on the brain, bleeding in my intestines, a ruptured windpipe and six broken ribs.

He says it is a miracle I am alive.

A Filipino nurse called Edith never stops coming in, checking my blood pressure. She changes my drip bag and asks how my pain is. If it's bad, she unclips something on the tube that goes from the drip bag into my arm, screws on a plastic syringe and slowly pushes the plunger. After that, clouds come over and the pain backs down.

A nurse called Fernando comes to change my other bags. The urine one is always full but the other one hardly ever has anything in it, because I can't eat.

Sometimes, because my body can't move, my mind flares up in anger. I am tired all the time, but sleep does not come. I tell Edith. Doctor Meyerling comes and says he will give me more sedatives.

My parents visit and my mother cries silently. I pretend I still can't speak. The next time, I manage to whisper hello. This brings my mother to life and she pulls a chair in close and clasps my hand, looking at me with concern.

"Aydin."

She looks at me for a while, thinking, and runs her hand up and down my forearm, which feels nice.

"You get better now, then when you're back home again, everything will be alright."

Father is sitting behind her mutely. He's not usually in the background like this.

"Okay," I manage.

"Is there anything you'd like us to bring?"

"Some of your börek."

She smiles and laughs, and she's crying.

"Of course, my pet."

They stay a while and father tells me about the business, but his voice is strained. His jaw tenses as he lets his eyes scan my body. He's angry about what happened to me, but he's hiding it.

When they leave, I spend a long time daydreaming of a life where they are happy.

Days and days pass in a continuum of morphine. Then one day, in walks Slobodan.

"Aydin!" he says, looking at my bandaged head, my body hooked to tubes and wires. He places his hand gently on my arm. I turn my eyes towards him. He smells of smoke and Slobodan.

"Hello Slobo," I whisper.

"What happened to you?"

"I got in a fight. How did you know I was here?"

"I went to the prison and they told me." Keeping his eyes on me and his hand on my arm, he pulls up a chair and sits, then looks at my tubes and the machines, then at my plaster-cast ankle.

"Broken ankle," I explain, smiling faintly. "Broken windpipe. Broken back. Broken everything. Don't know what's worse though: that, or the stuff they're giving me in here. Messes with your mind. I thought I was kicking drugs."

Slobodan shakes his head, his blue eyes searching me at a loss.

"Who you fight?"

"Lordowski," I reply. I look back up at the ceiling. My mind feels sludgy from the meds.

"Who's he?"

I turn my head towards him. "A gang leader. Big, ugly psycho. I managed to kick him, put him down, then his men did this to me. They said it was a message from Zola and the Master."

Slobodan's hand releases just enough for me to notice, then holds me again. His eyes are almost frighteningly pale blue.

"Go on…"

"They wanted to scare me off a deal I'd been offered, so they did this to me. The director had said if I testified against Zola and the Master, I'd be let out and they'd go to prison."

"Zola and your karate teacher had this done to you?"

I don't reply. He stares at me for a long time, thinking thoughts. Then he releases my arm suddenly, takes his tobacco pouch out and fishes out a lighter and a ready-made roll-up.

"Slobo," I rasp. "You can't smoke here."

"Please excuse me," he says as he blows out smoke, his Serbian accent coming out strongly, "but just now I am going to smoke cigarette."

He stands, turns away and pulls hard, then blows out a great jet of blue. I wish I hadn't told him now. He turns back to me.

"How did Zola know about deal?"

"I told another inmate. An addict. Thought he was my friend. He probably sold them the story. I should never have told him but I needed to talk, Slobo. I had nobody to talk to."

"And you accepted deal?"

"I didn't get the chance."

Slobodan is wearing his denim waistcoat and a navy and green chequered shirt with saggy sleeves. I notice a scar, just visible above his collar, maybe from his soldier days he never talks about. He looks calmly at me and drags hard on the shrinking roll-up, his other hand stuffed in his pocket. There are beads of moisture on his forehead.

"I'm just going to get better, Slobo," I say, "then take the deal and start a new life away from all this."

"Yes, you do that, get better," he replies, looking down at me then pressing the treacly stub of his roll-up into the wall and letting it drop. "Sorry for cigarette."

He puts his hand back on my arm briefly, but this time it's a cold touch.

"I'm going to go now Aydin. Sorry I can't stay."

He turns to open the door, leaving me with his reeking smoke and a hole where a farewell should have been.

My heart is pumping hard. He left so abruptly. I wanted him to stay. Seeing his back disappear through the door makes me realise how lonely I am.

The lights have been turned down so it must be night. They've put stickers on my chest again because I got another infection; I can feel it running around my veins like hot mercury. The peep, peep, peep of the monitor chases me urgently into a night of confused, wakeful dreams.

There has to be something I can do, not just rot here or die. I clench and unclench my fists, over and over. Then I tense my stomach, but that hurts my ribs. Still, I do it a bit more. Then I tense and relax my legs, over and over.

I'm going to do that regularly, fever or not. On my wall is a clock. On the hour and on the half, I'm going to exercise whatever bits of my body I can, lying here. I have to make my body stronger. And on the quarter hour, to fill in the time, I'll recite the verse of the Qur'an I know, because I'm having dark thoughts: I keep replaying the attack in my mind, making it worse than it was, so in my mind I die and my parents' hearts break and Uncle Mejid is never happy again. But when I recite, my mind smooths out.

Days have passed and the infection has subsided. I feel better. A short, stocky nurse with spiky blond hair called Claudia has started looking after me; she calls me "darling" and "love" and "sweetheart" in a nice, meaningless way. I can move quite a bit. I ask to reduce the morphine but the pains come back strongly, so I ask for it back. Its haze is one small thing to enjoy.

Out of the window, if I crane my neck, I can see a wet car park and a tree. An old woman is making her way slowly, slowly along a pavement using a walking frame, her head bowed.

Another week has passed. I can bend my legs now; I lift my feet and pull them towards me, then extend, like we did at the dojo. It hurts, but I keep going. I raise my hands above my head, then lower them, over and over. When Claudia or Doctor Meyerling comes in, I pretend to be lying still.

I pass my time reading comic books and watching an old television. Most days, my parents or my uncle and aunt visit. Other times I daydream of Steffi, but I can no longer picture her properly, which makes me anxious. I try and try to bring her face back to my mind's eye. I imagine us talking and walking through the park on a summer's day, free as birds, holding hands.

Weeks have passed. I can do quite a few things now – hobble slowly to the toilet with a frame, sit, stretch a bit. Claudia says she's amazed how quickly I've got better. But I've lost masses of weight. In the night when nobody's around and I can't sleep, I climb slowly and painfully out of bed, grasp my frame and do wobbly, slow little squats, pushing through the flashes of pain that go down my legs and around my ankle, then I go down to the floor, which takes ages, and do a single press-up, biting the pain, then I haul myself back into bed, sore and exhausted. Exercise helps me sleep. I need help sleeping, because most nights I drop off and wake up again almost straight away, my leg nerves on fire, blood hammering around my head, no longer sleepy at all. The doctor gives me different sleeping pills but they don't help, they just make me think bad things dressed up as good.

More weeks have gone by in a slow smear. I've been on an open ward for some time because I'm no longer at risk of infection. Everyone else here is much older than me. Next to me is Harald, an obese, white-skinned, white-bearded, white-haired old man with dementia. In the night he shouts out: "Edelheid! Edelheid! Come here. Bad dog." Things like that. Then: "Nurse? Help. Help." He says it almost as if he's talking to himself; not urgently. A nurse comes in and chastises him soothingly: "Harald, really, you must keep your clothes on, you can't go showing everythin' to everyone, there are ladies here," – meaning herself, since all the patients are men. She pulls his clothes back on, struggling to shift his great mass – "There we go, lie down, love. No – lie down. No, Harald, you have to lie down. What do you want to do? Do you want to get up? Okay. Lie down then." Then a long pause. "That's it, there we go, lie down. Breakfast is a bit later. You want some yoghurt? No? Okay? Well done Harald. Go to sleep now."

I keep the curtains drawn between us but I hear his every move. A few minutes after she's gone I hear his breathing getting heavy and his great, walrus frame shifting around on the creaking bed and crackling plastic mattress, then he struggles with something, grunting. Then silence. Then, barking out of the blue: "Edelheid! Bad dog. When I… when we…" then he tails off. Then suddenly: "Ingrid, will you come? No supper for me love." Then silence, just the beeping of some machine. I've asked to be moved away because he disturbs me, but they say they can't. They give me more relaxants.

Opposite me is a tiny, thin man who sleeps for much of the day, his bed tilted up, his tiny, wizened head perfectly centred, engulfed in a great white pillow. His body makes a little sausage beneath the blankets. When he's awake, he stares straight out of his gaunt eye sockets at nothing. I said hello to him yesterday as I returned from the toilet with my aluminium walking stick, and he jolted out of his stare and smiled a boy-ish grin showing missing teeth, then he told me how he was adopted after the First World War and went to fight in Italy in the Second, and how he hopes now to get better and go to live with his niece's family, also in Italy, "Not where we were stationed in the war, mind. Never want to go back there." He has pancreatic cancer. Then he goes back to staring. Then he sleeps.

A few days later I notice his head is turned to the side for once. His eyes are closed, his mouth slightly open, his skin grey. They wheel him out in his bed. Later a different man is wheeled in to take his place.

11

Woyak is in a hospital bed but it's in the prison so I know I'm dreaming, and I am looking desperately for Grünwald, then some warders are saying "Mesüt! Mesüt! Pack your bags Mesüt," then I wake up and two uniformed men are in the ward telling me I am well enough to go back to prison. Still wondering whether it's a dream, but realising it's not, I get shakily out of bed, making a show of my bad foot, but they just stand there and wait. There are papers to sign, then we get into a van and drive away. I'm in shock.

The prison gates swing slowly open and we drive through. I'm going straight to take the deal; there's no way I'm staying here, it's too harsh, there are too many drugs. If Zola and the Master come for me later, I'll just have to work out what to do.

"Deal? There's no deal, Mesüt," says the director, standing by his chair and looking out of the window like last time. He turns towards me.

"Your criminal friends Malodich and Lok are no longer the subject of investigations."

"Why not? They did all the things you say they did. I can testify to it."

He looks at me, a hint of amusement in his mouth and veiny eyelids.

"You're too late, Mesüt. Too late. Malodich and Lok were shot dead last month outside their club."

I stare at him. In my mind I see Yez the Kurd.

"Who did it?"

"Why do you ask?" retorts the director, examining me. I suddenly feel uneasy and cornered.

"It's just – it's a shock. Sorry. I knew them."

"Of course. Well," he says, turning towards the window again, "if you know anything about who might have done it, maybe there can be a deal after all. I mean, nobody will be sorry for those two, but justice still has to be done. We don't want anarchy on the streets of Berlin. The papers are calling us the Naples of the North. Me," he adds, looking back at me carefully, "I think it was another drug dealer. Word is, Zola crossed someone."

"If I could help I would," I say, looking away and trying to bury the image of Yez deep so I don't let it out. "I just want to get out of prison. I don't feel safe here after what happened to me."

"Oh, you shouldn't worry about that. No one will touch you now, you're the man who put Lordowski in hospital. You've earned a name for yourself in here, Mesüt."

"What? Lordowski went to hospital?"

"Internal bleeding," he says, peering at me. His jowls quiver ever so slightly. "He was spitting blood for days. They say you put him down with one kick. They say it was quite a performance."

The director smiles momentarily, looking at me with something almost like affection.

"You can go now, Mesüt. Keep your chin up and behave."

I rise unsteadily, grasping my stick and feeling dizzy. I turn and make to leave.

"You look like you're in some discomfort, Mesüt."

I hesitate but don't reply.

"Well, I'll make sure you keep getting your painkillers and sedatives, as many as you need. Behave yourself Mesüt," he says again. "And think about what I said. We're always grateful for information."

"They say," adds the director as I reach the door, "the perpetrator was a real professional. Just came, shot them and walked off without a word, right outside the club."

I don't turn around.

The director was right about my reputation. It's not that anyone says anything about what I did to Lordowski, but the way everyone behaves around me, it's like I'm a completely different person. Inmates greet me. One of them changed his course in the corridor to shake my hand as if he'd known me for ages. At the breakfast queue, people invite me to go in front of them. When I sit down, others sit next to me or near me.

Then one morning, Marlowe Grünwald sidles up in the queue.

"Aydin," he says brightly, perky and clear as if there were nothing between us. "We missed you."

I avoid his eyes. "Piss off Grünwald."

"I hear you got painkillers and stuff," he continues, sliding his tray along behind mine.

"Yeah, lots of them, so I won't be needing yours."

He lowers his voice: "If you have any to spare, let me know." He's speaking as if we're friends. How can he pretend like that? He goes on quietly in my ear. "I need painkillers and sleeping pills, my brother," he says. "I've got other things I can give you that'll make your stay easier. We're all in the same boat, Aydin. I'm just trying to help people."

I slide my tray along without answering, taking two yoghurts and an orange juice. I just want to get away from him.

Back in my cell I check my medicine bag: I have six boxes of sleeping pills and twenty-five foil strips of painkillers, ten to a strip. The director kept his word – they're giving me everything. It must be part of his approach. I turn them over. All that trouble I went to for a pill or two before, now I have hundreds. I take two painkillers and a sleeping pill and stuff my bag away.

The weeks go by. I sort electricals by myself now and the time goes by very slowly. All the while I think of my next painkiller dose. I take three at a time instead of two now, because it makes things a bit nicer. And three sleeping pills at night. Sometimes I think of Yez the Kurd shooting Zola and Lok, and I wonder whether he will come for me too.

For every fifty cables I sort, I reward myself with one painkiller, so once I've done a hundred and fifty, I take my next three pills. At first that means about three or four doses a day, so I speed up to make it five, because if I do more work, then it shouldn't harm me to take a few more pills.

At other times I fill my time with dreams of living and laughing with Steffi, but I've thought of her so much, now I can't really remember what she looks like. I've held so tight to her image that it's worn out and disintegrated, faded away, and all that remains is a kind of hollow frame with which I wear away the hours.

I think of my parents a lot. Maybe I've been unfair to them. They brought me up and looked after me.

When I was small, I was really happy at home. I try to work out when things changed and why. It would be better not to live with them. I think again about going to the hospice. Yez the Kurd would never know about the hospice. Not that it makes much difference, it's such a long time until I get out of here.

Grünwald keeps being friendly to me but he hasn't mentioned drugs again. I've been thinking. In a way he was right when he said drugs make things easier and I've been wondering why I got so angry at him. You have all this time in here, stretched out endlessly ahead of you, and the routine is so dull; it can't really be natural to stay sober in here. Everyone needs some escape. When you're free, you do things you enjoy in your spare time, like sports or drinking or seeing friends. In here, you need something too.

Later I decide – just as an experiment – to try out Grünwald's offer of something harder, just for a week, a bit like taking a little holiday. If I don't like it again, I'll stop and go back to the pills.

Next morning, Grünwald comes with his trolley and I sidle up to him.

"I've got pills," I say quietly. "What do you have for me?"

He replies without hesitation: "I'll give you a syringe for six pills. Same stuff as before."

A rush of adrenaline comes over me. It's this easy. "Sure," I say. "I've got thirty pills here, so you sort me out for the week, agreed?"

"Deal," he says, looking away and waving at someone across the canteen. He has so many friends.

Back in my cell I unwrap a syringe. I've got to survive in here somehow – I'll never make it all the way to the end without some relief. This is just for a week, then that should be enough. I press the point onto my vein, slide it beneath the skin. After all the needles at hospital, this is easy. I push the plunger and watch as the cylinder of clear liquid shortens and a cold sting creeps up my arm and disperses.

The world folds inwards, embracing me, welcoming me back into its delirious arms. Something cries on the breeze. As my vision folds up and I fall back without feeling, a sadness intermingles, seeping in through a dank cave, stalactites of sorrow, high above a blowhole from the wet and windy moors, I'm teetering on unsteady legs over a precipice of questions. A rescuer ought to have been there, and that would be me, but I just watch. A numb crust over everything keeps down the cry.

The first day is sweaty and disjointed. The second becomes twisted. Soon every inmate is stealing furtive glances at me. They must all be on the pills I give to Grünwald. I even saw Lordowski and he saw me but looked through me. His clique has shrunk to two.

The end of the week is coming. I've been thinking. I'm going to extend the syringes for two more weeks; a week is too short for a holiday. And three's a good number. Then I might quit.

The third week is an ocean of hallucinations and squalid things at night. I am intentionally unwashed. The warder spat in my cell and I didn't mind; I wanted to correct him because I am not worth hating, but I didn't think of it in time because my mind keeps going to something else on the way around. My parents came to visit. My uncle came and said, "Aydin? What's wrong with you?" I said nothing's wrong with me; I said that because I am experimenting with lying, just out of interest. I am planning to up my dose too, to do another two weeks on top but with more syringes, so that if I do quit it'll be on a high. I'll have to ask for more sleeping pills and painkillers, I'll say my kidneys hurt and my ankle hurts all night long, which is true.

People aren't letting me into the queue any more. Why would they? I couldn't fight if I tried. I'm just floating along the day, my rhythm the sudden rise and gradual fall of the dose, then I shiver all night but I don't require anything else and it's something I'm watching happen, my deterioration, the wasting of the muscles, the eye sockets. I might see how far I can make it go, which will mean extending further. Grünwald isn't going to mind. And the director won't mind. I tell the warders I don't want to see any more visitors.

I got more pills from the doctor, no questions asked. I've lost count of the weeks. I've lost count of the months. I'm doing two syringes now and my arm is strewn with puss-pimples and a few bigger scratches. I cough at night, spitting up blood and other bits of stuff, and I sweat and shiver and cry and groan. I wish it would go away, I wish I hadn't done this.

Then one day a warder comes in and throws a plastic bag of things onto my bed.

"Your time's up. Pack."

I freeze for a moment, then I stagger out into the corridor, petrified, looking for him, but he's gone. Where's Grünwald? I need syringes, I can't just leave here with nothing. Trembling, I pack the three I have and my squashed boxes of sleeping pills, but when I go in a daze to sign out, they fish the pills and needles out of my bag and take them away without comment.

"I need those," I protest weakly, but the guard slides me an envelope instead.

"Your prescriptions. Go to the chemist. Go and see a doctor. You're on your own now."

Uncle Mejid is waiting for me, his face worn with concern. I try to act normally, but the moment we step outside and I see the pitiless sky and my uncle's familiar car and feel the nausea and shivering washing back over me, I buckle at the knees and whimper and I stop in the car park and begin to sink down to the warm, pale grey tarmac which the sun looks down on and where black ants walk around all their lives, knowing where they're going. Uncle Mejid crouches down and puts his arm around my bony shoulder and I start to sob, juddering, a skeleton squatting among old vehicles. He holds me to his body and says nothing; I hear his breathing and smell his smell of sanity and home.

I watch an ant clambering. Behind the blank bulwark of my stare there is numb shame, anger and loathing. And I'm afraid of going into Berlin.

"Will you come back to us Aydin?"

It hurts my eyes to look at his. I cannot answer. The blank bulwark stops even my own thoughts; my mind is mute. I just lean against him. At least my breathing is rising and falling. At least my heart is beating.

PART III

12

Four weeks have passed since that day. I am sitting here in home-made rehab, confined to Uncle Mejid's flat, which I did agree to, but it's been a new kind of hell. The drug thoughts are a talon inside my chest, inside the whole of me, everywhere and nowhere, pulling inside my atoms day and night, broken only when my aunt and uncle appear with their kindness and meals; then the talon retracts but I still sense it there like grit in every fibre of my mind. I want to go out, but I'm scared to and I'm not allowed to anyway.

Uncle Mejid closes the door quietly behind him and sits carefully on a sofa. I hug my knees, prop my chin on them and rock gently backwards and forwards, looking at the floor.

"How are you, Aydin?"

I shake my head and stay quiet. How many ways are there to say you're not well? Uncle Mejid sighs.

"There's something I've been wanting to tell you," he says. "About your grandparents. I'm not supposed to…"

I look up at him. "Please do."

He stays silent for what seems like an age.

"They were important people. From an important family," he says, looking at me measuredly. "If you go back a few generations, they were descended from the sultans."

I put my feet down on the floor and stare at him.

"When the rule of the sultans ended, your grandparents fought against the modern Turkish state which replaced it, because they believed it was against Islam."

Uncle Mejid sighs again.

"They were killed. Your father and I… our parents just disappeared. But your mother," he says, faltering, "she was made to watch hers being executed."

He drops his face and shields his eyes with one hand, sobbing silently.

"She was just a girl."

Hot tears spring to my eyes. My mother. All wrapped up in her scarves and pins and thick coats.

"Your father and I," continues Uncle Mejid, wiping his eyes, "were sent here to Germany, and so was your mother. When she and your father met and married, they never talked about what happened and they decided not to tell you or your brother. It was a pact that just got made, because it was too upsetting."

Later that day, Uncle Mejid says that he and Aunt Selma will be out all evening. Without telling them, I'm slipping out to go to Café Abgang, nerves on edge, a pulse in my ears. I feel like somebody different after what he told me. I feel like someone with a past stretching back to another world. But I'm also afraid. I look at anyone who appears up ahead, checking for short Kurdish men with big shoulders. I avoid the street where Yez lives.

I need to see Slobodan, even if I don't drink or anything. I have to see him, to tell him I'm out, tell him what I've just learned. And if he's there, maybe I can stay distracted from the grit in my mind. Maybe Slobodan knows about Yez too, and about Zola and the Master getting shot. I want to ask him everything.

The pull of beer is so strong, so beautifully strong. How a drink would help a day like today. Maybe beer is better than drugs? I picture korn, its clear liquid creeping up the sides of the little glass and scorching my throat. The friendly sound of people I don't know. Waves from people I do. All that jumbled up comfortable life I took for granted. Deadpan barman Jürgen and his easy-flowing tab. Music. Wolfgang the Pigtail and his powder lines that banish cares. Pool. Pinball. Roll-ups on the bench. All the feelings of reckless abandon I've spent the last four weeks trying hopelessly to get out of my head: now I'm walking towards the place where it all happens. Every person I approach and pass, once I've checked they're not Kurdish, I begin to ask myself whether they're wondering about me, ex-convict, addict, man with nothing, no resistance, a hollow core – descendent of sultans.

Café Abgang is in sight. When I arrive, Slobodan's not there. Jürgen's pulling a beer and looking up at me over his oblong glasses, the kind that so many Germans wear. Turks don't wear them – unless they're the sort of Turks who've become totally German. He looks at me for longer than usual, thinking, pulling the handle. He places the glass down to let the first draft settle, takes a glistening empty glass and points to it, raising his eyebrow at me.

I give the thumbs-up, hating my own lack of resistance. He places the glass beneath the tap and pulls the handle, his sagging, tanned arm flexing a bit in his polo shirt. I sit on a barstool and watch. He places a coaster on the bar in front of me and the tall glass of amber onto it.

"Has Slobo been here?" I ask.

Jürgen peers at me again over his German, oblong glasses, looking at me for longer than usual, saying nothing, then he swallows and looks back at the beer. It's odd, because he never looks at anyone for long, never stops to talk for long, a man of brusque brisk ways, serving, doing, moving. But now he comes over to me and takes his glasses off, pockets them in his shirt, leans his forearms on the bar and shakes his head.

"Slobo's dead, Aydin."

Slobo's dead? What can he mean by saying Slobo's dead? I picture Slobo in his flat with his bulldog, rolling a cigarette. He must be there or somewhere else. He can't possibly be dead.

"No way."

"Yes, Aydin. He did it to himself," says Jürgen.

Jürgen is actually a handsome man, I just realised, and a kind man.

"What – how do you know?"

"He left a note, apparently."

He shrugs and looks at me. I still don't really believe him.

"His Serbian friend said he always had issues because of things that happened in the army."

I start to feel weak and quite sick, then a whole surge of horror and terror wells up, but I keep it in. I look at the beer in front of me, sickening, disgusting yellow fluid that belongs to someone else, which I feel like sweeping off the bar and onto the floor, but I don't.

"My wife says she's not surprised he did it," says Jürgen. "She says he was never a happy man. They say things happened to him in Serbia."

Sweat rushes to my brow and I begin to swallow again and again. I twist around to look at the people sitting at tables in the gloomy room with its dim, nicotine stained lamps. A man I vaguely know sees me and waves then resumes hushed conversation with his friend.

Jürgen is facing me, arms on the bar. He puts his glasses back on and looks at me over their rims, then points at my beer and raises an eyebrow. I look away and shake my head. He picks it up and pours it down the stainless steel sink behind him. That was my last ever beer he just poured away.

"How can I contact his Serbian friend?" I ask in a quavering voice.

"No idea. Nobody knows him." He laughs a sad laugh. "We never really knew Slobodan in that way. He had a girlfriend who used to come here, but that was years ago. They split up."

"Okay," I say. "I'm gonna go. Sorry about the beer."

"No problem," he says, smiling with wrinkly eyes. "Don't take it hard. And look after yourself – you don't look well."

As I make to leave, Wolfgang the Pigtail comes in through the door in his sleeveless, black leather jacket.

"Wolfgang!"

"Hi," he replies, but he doesn't stop. He's always going somewhere.

"Wolfgang," I say after him. "Can I see you a minute?"

He looks back at me for a moment then says yes, so I follow him through to the pool room.

"Wolfgang, did you hear about Benjamin Lok and Zola Malodich?"

"Of course I did." He stands facing me with his hands buried deep in his pockets.

"Do you know who did it?"

"Why?"

"Was it a Kurdish guy called Yez?"

Wolfgang looks at me. I can tell he's thinking about whether to talk to me.

"Because if it was," I continue, "I know why."

"So what if you know?" he asks.

"Nothing. But," and I lower my voice because there are two men playing pool – "I was there when they crossed Yez. They said he had cheated them."

Wolfgang takes a step forward so we're standing very close.

"Whatever you know, you should keep it quiet," he says slowly and quietly.

"That's why I'm asking you. Because Yez said he would remember me too and come and find me. I was the driver."

Wolfgang huffs a little laugh and looks disbelievingly at me.

"Everyone thinks it was Yez," he says, "because Yez was mouthing off against Lok and Malodich for months, making threats. But now," he says, looking around furtively, "Yez is crying that he never did it." Wolfgang takes a little step back from me. "Nobody knows who did it."

"I – I just don't want Yez coming after me."

"Well," says Wolfgang, "Yez is Kurdish, so he's not going to like you from the start, is he? But then again, now Lok and Malodich are dead, why would he worry about a little driver?" and he shrugs.

I feel out of my depth.

"What about Slobodan, Wolfgang? What happened? What did he do that for?"

"I dunno, Aydin," he says.

It's the first time he's ever said my name. I wasn't even sure he knew it.

"But he was talking about you a lot when you were in prison. He said he saw you in hospital and that you were an addict and that Malodich and Lok had you punished. Is that right?"

I hesitate. "Yes."

"Yeah. And he lost his little brother to drugs, and you were his little brother too. Maybe he was torn up."

I stare at him.

"Anyway," says Wolfgang, "it's no use guessing. He's gone now. And I'm going too."

He pats my arm.

"See you."

I stand on the threshold of Café Abgang and look out at the cold, empty street where parked cars sleep beneath dust and leaves. The benches are long gone because winter has come. Mulch lies in the gutter. Slobodan's gone, the Master's gone, Zola's gone, the summer's gone. All gone, gone, gone. I sit on Café Abgang's long, low windowsill with its blistered paint. Behind me, muffled through the frosted glass, drinkers and music jangle on. In front of me, the city, humming endlessly, never sleeping. I will never go back in there behind me to drink. Ever. The murmuring world behind the glass is now a world for others – the ones I hear inside behind the window, debating, clinking glasses with their droning, muffled music and bursts of odd laughter.

It's the same with the world of drugs. I am not going back there, however much it pulls. And I am not going back to the underworld either, the underworld that's all around me here in this neighbourhood, across this city, in grubby flats like Yez's where deals are done.

Damn to all the things that took me into that world. Damn Zola. Damn the Master. He used to tell me to fight and not hold back. I will fight his world, he can be sure, watching me from whatever place he's in.

All these thoughts come pouring upon me all at once, clear as day, flushing out dirt. I have allowed myself to be pushed around. Pushed around by others. Pushed around by my own cravings. After the shock of all I've seen and the sickness about all I've done, I feel like I'm standing alone, unsteadily, deep inside myself. But it's a place that could be my own.

There are things I'm going to need to do. First, Yez the Kurd. I can't live looking out for shadows. I get to my feet and walk towards where he lives and begin to think of what to do. I need to draw a line with him. I need to make things right. I need to apologise. I know it's not the underworld way, but I'm not an underworld person. I'll have to think of my own way.

But as I think about it, I realise it will take more thought, so I turn around and head back to Uncle Mejid's flat.

There, I wash for the prayer. The prayer needs to come before everything if I'm really going to start afresh. Five times a day to keep me straight.

Early the next morning I tell Uncle Mejid I'm going out to the shops, which he accepts without comment. I'm still shivering and shaking from the drugs, but it's as if it's in a different room somewhere. The room I am occupying is clear, the place where I know who I am. Unsteady, but clear. I'll have to keep busy though.

The air on the street is fresh and full of the smells of baking and the sounds of people going to work and out on errands like me. At the pet shop on the big boulevard I buy a kitten in a plastic cage. It looks angry and afraid. I try to sooth it, but it hisses.

Outside Yez the Kurd's building, I ring the bell and it buzzes open straight away. I climb the stairs. Nothing has changed in here. It still smells of cats. My heart is hammering and I'm afraid. The kitten mews desperately.

I ring the doorbell. Soon the peephole flickers just like it did before, but this time there is a long silence.

Then the door opens onto the latch chain and two accusative eyes beneath thick eyebrows peer out through the gap.

Yez looks at me long and hard.

"What you want?"

"I've brought you a new cat, Yez."

I hold the box up so he can see the mewing kitten through the bars. His eyes dart at it, then lock back onto me.

"And I'm sorry for what we did."

"No," he says. "I don't want a new cat."

His eyes retreat and the door begins to close.

"Yez!"

It stays ajar, but his eyes do not reappear.

"I'm sorry."

"Go away," comes his voice, then the door closes gently and clicks shut.

The kitten mews and mews. I descend the stairwell.

Down on the street, young Turks and Germans going places, cars queuing, displays of fruit and vegetables teetering colourfully above the pavement. Back at the pet shop I buy some cat food, and back at the flat I show Uncle Mejid the kitten and open its little cage door. It comes out nervously, its little yellow eyes scanning everything fearfully, its ears twitching at every sound, its fur dark grey and soft like dandelion clocks.

Later I think of Steffi. She'll know about the shooting of Lok and Malodich. And I want to see her again.

In the evening, I make my way to the U-Bahn. It's

a straight ride to Steffi's, no changes. Slobo never used to ride the U-Bahn; he had something against it. Now he's killed himself. Where's the sense in that? I get out at Voltastrasse and jog to her place to keep warm, passing the silent streets I know so well. The name by her bell is Schmidt, which could be her or it could be her flatmate. It doesn't matter to me now. I ring it. There is a long silence. I ring again and look through the names on the bell array. Holst. Ramelow. Konstanin. Müller. Klein. Normal, working people. Then a clattering comes through the intercom and a girl's voice speaks quietly.

"Yes?"

"Steffi, this is Aydin."

There is a long pause, the crackling of interference in the background. Then a clatter and it goes silent. I wait. I wait more. Nothing happens. Then the door buzzes and my heart jumps up and I push the door open with a click.

I'm bounding up the stairs three at a time, ignoring the pain in my ankle and the grit and the talon in my mind.

The door is ajar and Steffi peeps out. Her eyes look softer without make-up and her black hair is much longer than it used to be. She checks me out for a moment then undoes the latch chain and lets me in. She stands there and waits while I take off my shoes, then we look at each other for a few seconds, then we both smile, then we kind of embrace, but just touching cheeks, ever so lightly, and I breathe in her gentle scent and I'm careful not to hug her much, then I move away. My heart is battering my ribcage so hard, I think she'll hear it.

"Come in," she says, leading me into the flat. I follow, watching her shoulders. On the table is a small, black, octagonal mug which she takes away and places by the sink among other unwashed items.

"Tea? Coffee?"

"Sure, a tea would be nice."

Shaking, I sit on her black futon and focus on the walls while she clanks around in the kitchenette. It feels like my first time here, even though I've been so many times. On one wall is a large, framed poster, six feet long, a disorderly arrangement of coloured blocks and other random shapes receding into a horizon; on another are two framed concert posters, one of an American and one of a German rock group. None of that was here before. The flat smells of coffee and carpets. I think it's been repainted.

She gives me a mug and sits at the table. I clasp its warmth and sip.

We look at each other tenderly, holding back. Then she speaks very softly.

"I heard you were in prison."

"I was," I exhale, blowing steam from the top of the cup. "Got out four weeks ago."

"I'm so sorry."

"No," I laugh, "It was a learning experience."

She smiles, then she looks at my head.

"What happened to you?"

"I got beaten up. I was in hospital."

She puts her hand over her mouth and searches my outline, examining my head, my body. She must see that I'm shaking. I try not to let her see it.

"I'm a lot better now though. I almost died."

I sip my tea and change the subject.

"And Zola and Benjamin Lok," I say, watching her reaction. "They got shot?"

She looks away out of the window at the black tenement backs. There is a long silence in which I hear only my heart pounding. I can't see her face properly because of some long hair hanging down.

"So many thing have happened," I continue, uneasy that I can't see her. "Yesterday at the bar, I found out my best friend committed suicide."

"Oh no," she says, turning her head and looking at me with wide eyes, but there are already tears in them, which throws me. Her face is altered in some way I can't make out; maybe less flawless, but no less captivating. Her eyes, I remember now, used to be immaculate sapphires set in silver. Now they're pearling dew in the morning.

"So many people have died," I say. "I just wanted to see you were alright. And I needed to talk."

She smiles at me and it sinks in that she's really, actually here, in the flesh, not just in my worn-out imagination. I take in the face that I'd forgotten. She wipes away a tear and in one stroke moves a long strand of hair from out of her face. When I used to come here, we'd just take off our clothes, hardly talk. It's so different now. All I want to do is talk; her body is out of bounds.

"So," I say, hesitating, "do you... do you know what happened to Zola and Lok?"

Steffi looks down at her feet and her hair falls either side of her face. She's wearing jeans and a grey vest. Her arms and shoulders are tanned and gently muscular, just as I remember them, except her assuredness has gone. Without her glittery make-up her lips are real. I can see so many emotions in her, even when her head is hanging. It's as if she's peeled off a mask. Her fingernails are unvarnished, a shade pinker than her bronze, slender fingers. Her eyes look ever so slightly oriental.

She and glances up at me and sniffs, wiping away another tear.

"Sorry," I say, "I didn't want to upset you, I just wanted to make sure you're alright. I can go."

"No! Please don't."

She looks out at the tenements again. There are lights on in some windows, others are black. A tear drips from her chin.

Then she drops her head again, puts her hand across her eyes and begins to cry in bursts, her shoulders shaking. I get up and kneel before her and embrace her in what way I can, awkwardly, the top of her head pushing into my chest. She weeps and weeps.

"It's okay," I say.

She goes on crying and I stroke her arm and lean my head onto the back of hers. There's a hot smell of tears and saliva. Eventually she raises her head and I let her go, still crouching in front of her.

She looks straight at me, her eyes red, an angry, exposed person I hardly know.

"Your karate master was my father."

I frown. I don't know what to think about that. I don't even want to think about that. The Master was her father? She hangs her head again towards me, so I lean in again and hold her, but even more carefully this time. I stare through one of the coloured blocks on the poster in front of me; my eyes focus beyond the vanishing point. I thought I had been down in a deep hole of suffering. But she is further down than me.

Eventually, once she's stopped crying, we move to the couch and begin to talk – for ages. She tells me about her father, the Master. How he was not there when she was growing up, how she went looking for him as a teenager and found him at Zola's, how he treated her like a princess there, how he gave her all the drinks she wanted, then drugs too, how she was the queen of the club, how men would ask about her, how he used to suggest talking to this one or that one, how things started to happen, how she eventually realised money was changing hands... how it was too late to get out, how she'd become scared of him because of the things she saw him doing to people and the way everyone talked about him.

And then, one night, while I was in prison, a tall, broad man in a balaclava walked up to the club as Zola's car pulled up and shot Zola and her father as they got out, then he walked away down the road and turned into a side street and disappeared.

Then I tell her about myself. How I fell into her father's world. Driving for Zola. Yez the Kurd and his threat. Getting caught. Prison. The pills. The syringes. About praying then giving up, then starting again. About Heinrich von Weser. Lordowski. The hospice. Peter with leukaemia and the way he loved things. Aunt Carla. Woyak. The testifying deal. The fight with Lordowski. Hospital. The injuries, the pain, the painkillers, then the gripping, sick addiction. I tell her how Uncle Mejid got me to agree to stay in his flat so I would come off drugs, about my grandparents, and I tell her about going to Abgang, then the news of Slobo's suicide, then about giving up drink and drugs sitting out there on the windowsill, even though they still gnaw somewhere inside me; how I'm afraid I might slip back if I'm in the city.

She holds out a hand, and I lean over and sink my

head down into her lap and just lie there. Steffi is quiet for a long time, her abdomen going up and down beneath my heavy head. She strokes my hair gently, gently.

Then she shifts around a bit, seeming uncomfortable. I sit up. She's looking straight ahead, thinking, then she speaks.

"That place you mentioned. The care home."

"Yes?"

"You should still do that. You should go there."

I stay quiet and think about it.

"Maybe," I say.

"No, not maybe. Definitely," she says. "You need to get out of Berlin. You need to go there."

"I don't even know where it is," I protest. But I already know she's right.

She's quiet for a moment.

"Just go. Find out where it is and go."

13

I'm alone in a hot, stuffy train carriage leaving the outskirts of Berlin. It rocks and tocks over points, rumbling at jogging pace past Spandau's staring concrete edifices. Patches of pointless land lie locked down by winter's frosty hand. A man in a thick coat and fur hat is walking his dachshund by the lines; he picks it up and it looks up at him hopefully; he slaps its nose hard. I frown and turn to look as we pass them. The dog still gazes up at him with longing eyes. Sterile factories wait silently beneath the frigid fog. Lamp posts line the tracks as the train approaches the border crossing into the East. Away to either side stretches the grubby Wall and its empty watchtowers that stand sentinel over an abandoned strip of land. One watchtower is right by the track; on it stands a soldier, leaning with folded arms on a frozen railing, looking out over the structures. Perhaps he has not been told it's all over. I wave at him and he looks down at me but does not respond.

I'm out of Berlin now, clickety-clacking into the flat, sorry land of Brandenburg. A dense fog is on everything. An occasional building looms momentarily out of it then is swallowed up in the train's clunking, swirling eddy. Stones and sleepers go by in a soporific blur; further away there's an embankment and then intermittent fields, large, dark pine forests and forlorn allotments on the edges of towns where the plaster on the buildings is flaking and crumbling. There are old bullet holes in some of the walls.

Three quarters of an hour later I'm stepping down onto a deserted platform and into the grip of a freezing mist. The station's mouldering signboard is inscribed in Gothic letters. This, said the man at the library, is the stop for the hospice. But the hospice is far from here so I will need to take a bus.

"No busses on Sunday."

The man in the ticket office doesn't even look at me through the glass.

"No taxis either. It's Sunday, hadn't you heard?" He takes his pen and taps a calendar stuck up on the glass, this time looking at me through bottle lenses.

"Do you know of a hospice nearby run by a Count von Weser?"

"Count who?" he looks at me accusatively. "Never heard of him."

I stare at him. I think he does know.

"Well do you know of any hospice then?"

"No."

"A man at our library said it was around here."

"Well what are you asking me for then?" he says, returning to his tabloid in his heated cubicle.

I walk away. Outside the station I unwrap my map, its pages stuck together. It has been largely stripped of detail by its East German publishers, in the days of the Wall when they didn't want people to know too much. I don't feel sure about how to read maps either, but if the man at the library is right then the hospice is the tiny grey mark some distance out of the bigger grey patch which is this drab little town – in the direction the train went – and then down a side road. I begin to walk.

Ten minutes and I'm at the edge of the town where the fog is a degree colder. My ankle is aching and my scalp is hurting. I should've asked my aunt for a hat. At least I told them where I'm going and they were more or less glad. After a while of walking I come alongside a plantation of spruces whose dark interior looks inviting beneath its frosted thatch, so I climb a fence, enter its embrace and walk quickly along between the straight ranks of trees, my footsteps noiseless on the soft bed of needles save the muffled snap of a part-buried twig, the air silent as if all sound has been sucked out. There is not a living creature in here. Eventually I lose sight of the road completely; I press on for a while then bear right to intercept it again. The forest changes into a random plantation of smaller firs so I bear a bit further right and continue; later I turn even further right but I still cannot see the road.

Instead I reach the edge of the plantation and find myself looking out over a ploughed field whose frozen ruts stretch away into the mist. I have my hands buried in my pockets but my fingers are throbbing from the cold. My ankle stings.

A hundred metres into the field and I feel angry with myself for trying to walk on this brick-hard ploughed mud. My left foot breaks through some ice into some slime and is caked; I can't feel those toes now and I grazed my hand in the fall. The aches and pains of my prison injuries are all brought out by the cold.

Everything is completely still. A fenced ditch appears out of the murk and some way along to the left is a small, rickety-looking tower with a shattered wooden platform on top. I climb its jagged, ramshackle steps and sit on frosty, lichened planks in the gloom. Beside me are three recently used bullet cases and an empty cigarette box. If only they had left me one. A rook crarks at me from the fence below.

I climb down and follow the fence and ditch. The freezing fog is so thick now; anything could be beyond it. I could have passed a house. I could have passed the hospice and I wouldn't know.

After some time it grows eerily dark in front of me, then black fingers and arms reach out from the mist: the pines of another plantation.

I cross the tractor ruts of a broad firebreak where the darkness lifts momentarily before plunging me back into the eerie mists of the next battalion of trees; these are younger, denser and lower, and I have to stoop to avoid their needly limbs. The carpet here is softer and springier.

Now I'm standing at the end of a field where the mist is thinning. I climb another fence. A sweet, pungent smell wafts up into the frozen air; manure has been spread here not long ago, but now it is frozen.

At the other side of the field are the desolate up-pointing skeletons of birches and behind them the tangled frames of bare oaks, stock-still in their creeping dance. Beyond them is a black, glassy lake vanishing silently into the fog, its edges embroidered with crystalline ice. I poke the ice with a stick; it breaks away in floes. A well-worn footpath, bejewelled with ice crystals, runs alongside the lake so I follow it until it veers away from the water's edge.

Somewhere out on the water beyond my sight there is a splash. I peer towards it and see a hint of a straight line among the reeds, then a silhouette, then the stern of a small rowing boat, half in the water, half out. I prod it and it complains with a creak; wafer-thin ice hisses and ruptures around the hull. Its oars lie inside. I step gingerly on board.

I push the boat out into the lake, making undulations on the glass. But it is not a lake; it is a sluggish river: I see foliage on its far bank now; leafless creepers drooling from a crippled trunk; reeds; an overhanging bare branch; a willow void of green, hanging its disappointed fingers in the water, waiting.

The oars clunk and clatter in their iron gates. I'm smoothing away down along a boiling current now. The river narrows until overhanging trees almost touch and I can stop rowing and drift, then it opens out and the woods fade and fade away to the sides until I am sitting on another silent black mirror in the fog. A bird coos somewhere to my right and another chuck-chucks in reply, then there is silence. Later, a large splash. I take the oars again and row, following my shivering instincts.

The sky may be getting darker, I can't tell. At least I'm warm from rowing and my ankle is thankful for the break. It's half an hour before I finally spot the outlines of reeds and bushes in the mist and it's definitely darkening now: the air is growing sadder, from a watery to a stony blue. The boat slides to a halt at the edge. I step out into mud up to my shins, ice-cold water seeping into my shoes, and flounder to the frozen bank.

The sky above is now like dark denim and the fog has become a freezing, low-lying mist; I can see some stars. I am walking fast along the ruts made by a tractor, and now I come out into a small road and turn right. I have to keep going to block out the pain in my frozen feet. My whole body is beginning to judder and I can't prevent it; I breathe in gasps and cannot stop for the cold. I begin to run. I'm trying to stem the panic and trying not to think what might happen to me now that night has come and I'm completely lost. The room at my uncle's will be warm right now, my aunt's food hot.

I come to a driveway that leads into some woods, so I take it. Somewhere up ahead I see a pinprick of light. It is a house and outside is a small trailer and a scooter with only one wheel. Further behind, showing through the trunks of the trees, are the reflections of the river's black water again. I stumble to the door, shaking, and knock loudly.

A light appears in the window above the door and I hear a woman calling something to someone inside. Then it opens. Standing there, taken aback by my wretchedness, is a young, short, mousy woman with a plain face and thin nose. She is wearing a green three-quarter length skirt and a baggy pullover with muted brown and yellow horizontal stripes.

"Good evening," she says, looking more evenly now and with a touch of suspicion. "Can I help you?"

"Y-yes," I stammer, my jaw juddering uncontrollably. "I'm lost. I've lost my way. Sorry. Can you help me?"

She looks down at my muddy feet.

"You'd better come in."

I remove my shoes, trying my best to stay standing, but then my legs fail me and I sink to the floor, sitting. There is a smell of cooking coming along the little corridor.

"Olaf," she calls. "We've got a visitor. He's not very well."

Someone acknowledges her from further inside the house.

I pull myself back to my feet, nerves jangling, and she leads me down the corridor and into a living room.

"Sit, rest. Make yourself comfortable," she says courteously.

I try to conceal my shaking, but I can't.

"Are you alright?" she asks, looking at me with concern.

"I g-got very cold, t-too cold. I'm sorry."

"I'm not surprised. Who'd be out on a night like this? Olaf? Come. We've got a visitor."

In walks a tall, lanky man with round spectacles wearing a sleeveless cardigan over a shirt with baggy arms. He has a disorganised beard and is balding.

"Hello," I say, rising unsteadily. "Thank you for letting me in. I'm lost."

Olaf saunters across to me and shakes my hand, then winces.

"You're freezing," he says.

"I know. I didn't bring gloves."

"What are you doing in these parts on a Sunday night?"

"I'm looking for the hospice of Heinrich von Weser."

"Oh. You've strayed quite far. Did you walk here?"

"Y-yes," I say, my jaw refusing to calm down. "From the train station."

"The station? That's miles away."

Olaf sits opposite me; the woman, standing at the doorway, asks:

"Would you like something hot?"

"I won't say no," I reply.

She nods and disappears.

"Thank you so much," I say. "I was getting scared."

"I bet," smiles Olaf. "Where are you from?"

"Berlin."

"Well, welcome."

The room is snugly furnished with items that look thirty or forty years old: block-like armchairs upholstered in striped green and cream velour, a Formica coffee table with a little laced runner on it, a glass display cabinet containing odd plates and trinkets, a forlorn picture of a mountain hung off-centre on an off-white wall. In the corner is a tall, tiled stove emitting so much heat it almost makes me faint. Various old lamps around the room give off dim yellow light. The carpet has a swirly green pattern.

The woman returns with a plastic tray on which lies a white napkin and on top of that a low, wide bowl of steaming green soup.

"Thank you," I say, and take a mouthful; it tastes

233

of peas. The woman sits in the chair next to the man. They watch me eating.

"So what're you going to do at von Weser's place?" asks the woman. "I'm Gretchen by the way, and this is Olaf."

"Aydin," I reply, placing down my spoon and putting my hand to my chest. "I'm going to work there. I worked there before."

An infant squawks somewhere in the house; Gretchen gets up.

"I'm just thinking how to get you there," says Olaf drumming his fingers. "Our car's out on loan 'til tomorrow morning."

Gretchen reappears holding a toddler which stares at me and blinks big blue eyes in the light of the living room. His blond hair is a tangle and he is dangling a teddy bear by one leg.

"Say hello to the visitor," coos Gretchen, peering lovingly into his face. He gazes blankly at me then turns his head away quickly and looks at the far wall.

"Shy boy," says Olaf, waving at the child. "I was just telling Aydin our car's out, so we're housebound."

"Well we can put out a mattress if you don't mind sleeping on the floor," she says.

"That's so kind. I don't know what to say. Thank you."

A bed has been made for me on the floor and I have been left alone. We talked a while about the river, whose rowing boat it might have been that I took (Olaf said he knows), the fall of the Wall, life in East Germany and their tousled little son. When they go to bed, I do my prayers in the corner. The ticking, clicking stove is still giving off some heat and I open the window, letting icy air trickle down behind the curtain and seep along the carpet to where I am now lying on top of the bedding, staring at the woodchip ceiling; I shiver and get up to close it again, then fall back onto my bed, draw up the covers and think restful thoughts: There are no drugs here in this simple place. My eyelids slowly close. If Steffi were here with me, we could talk on into the night. I imagine that for a long time and eventually drop off into a smooth, dream-free sleep.

14

Olaf is driving me to the hospice in his clattering car. It would have been much too far to walk. There's nobody at the gates. After a minute or two of wondering what to do we open them ourselves and drive in. The gravel's crunch is muffled by leaves and winter's wet; the rich greens of my last visit have gone and the grounds look naked: lattice trees stand against a gloomy sky. Sleet falls diagonally.

Nobody is working the garden either; nobody is around at all in fact. The rose bushes along the front are spindly and bare save a single white, tattered flower which jiggles in the frigid breeze. I see lights in two windows downstairs and one above; the rest are dark.

Olaf's car splutters and coughs as I wait at the top of the steps and knock again. After a good few minutes it opens and the butler stands before me. Olaf's engine revs, he waves, and he pulls away in a cloud of dirty smoke.

Minutes later I'm sitting in the salon and in hobbles Heinrich von Weser, propped on the arm of the butler. He has lost a lot of weight. Between his neck and his short collar there is a wide, dark gap, his eyes are sunken and his cheeks hollow; his trousers are baggy and not very clean. He is supported between a stick which wobbles in one hand and the butler on the other. But what has really changed is his voice.

"Aydin," he croaks, so quietly I can hardly hear. "How wonderful to see you."

He walks slowly towards me and I rise to my feet. His hand is still strong, though I feel his bones much more beneath flaccid skin. He drops into a feather armchair, sending up dust.

"Please, sit."

"What's happened to you, Count von Weser?"

He laughs weakly.

"Bone cancer."

"Oh no."

I glance at his thin frame and wonder what bone cancer means.

"I'm so sorry to hear that."

He lifts his hand and looks around the room. "It's all this. Bit off more than I can chew."

"But what about all the people you look after?"

"A few are still here. Two die-hards."

I feel blank and cold. The room doesn't seem to be heated.

"Andreas' partners won't release any more money because they say the risk is too great in the new environment. Nobody knows how things are going to develop out here in the East. Truth be told, what they're really worried about is investing in me, given the state I'm in."

"I'm so sorry."

"No, no. It's probably for the best. I mean – look at me. I'm afraid there's not much fight left in me." He smiles. His eyes still twinkle in their gaunt sockets.

"I've come to work for you," I say, "if you'll have me."

"There's not much here for you I'm afraid. The only patients left are non-payers who we're just caring for as best we can until their time comes."

It seems an effort for him to speak.

"Is Peter still here?" I ask anxiously.

"No, Peter died, dear boy."

I stare at the old man, lost for a response, my head numb. I think back to when I wheeled Peter in the busy garden. A ten-year-old kid. He'd barely started living. And now this old man in front of me might be dying too.

Hot tears spring to my eyes. I cover my mouth and look at von Weser and try to speak, but my mind is racing ahead of me. My jaw trembles and the room goes crystalline through tears.

"I cried too," says von Weser. "There was something about Peter."

I wipe my face with my sleeve and pull myself together. "Well," I say. "I came here to work for you and you don't need to pay me, I'll work anyway. It's what I want to do."

Heinrich von Weser looks at me for a moment. He seems to want to say something, but then changes his mind and twists his torso towards the door, which opens. The butler steps in.

"We'd better make up a room for Mr Aydin," says von Weser. "Alright Anton? Please prepare the guest room."

"Certainly Sir."

"What about Aunt Carla?" I ask, drying my face again. "How is she?"

"Oh," he smiles. "She'll probably outlast me. I might not survive this." Count von Weser rises unsteadily, turns and reaches for his stick with a shaking hand. "Given me such a tremor, it has." He pauses, holding the arm of the chair, his back facing me. It is humped and his jacket has space in it.

"You can go and see her if you want. She liked you, kept mentioning you," he says, still facing away from me and beginning to move. "You know the way."

I am standing outside Aunt Carla's door. I have been here for a couple of long minutes, but it's silent from within. I knock tentatively and cautiously open it.

"Who is it?" comes a strong, anxious voice from the semi-darkness.

"It's Aydin Mesüt."

"Who? Heinrich? Andreas? Are you there?"

I enter and stand in the middle of the room, my eyes adjusting. It is as if she has not moved since I was last here.

"Aydin, the Turkish man from the prison. Do you remember me?"

"Turkish? Turkish? I don't know anyone Turkish. Come closer, let me see you, strange man." She beckons and I step up before her.

"Ahh!" she exclaims. "Of course I remember you. Aydin the Conqueror," and she beams and shakes a shrivelled fist energetically. "Aydin the Conqueror. Did you ever find out about your ancestors?"

"Yes, I…"

"Sit down, sit down. Why are you standing there like that? Pull up a chair if there is one. The Russians left me with nothing."

I sit.

"I did find out about my ancestors. My uncle told me a bit about them last week when I was staying with him. They go back a long way," I laugh. "Right back to the sultans."

"I told you! Well, I'm pleased you followed my advice because nobody else does. They all consider me quite mad."

"I've come here to work," I tell her. "I got side-tracked when I left last time. But now, well, Count von Weser says he can't accommodate me because there's no money."

"No money? What nonsense. Since when did that matter? We lived on stale bread and boiled boots in the war and we're still here. You should stay." She scrutinises me then adds: "You look thin, Aydin. Have you been looking after yourself?"

"Not really."

She huffs.

"Count von Weser told me about his health," I continue, "and the hospice running down."

"Oh yes, oh yes, poor man. It's his life's work. All he cares about. It was his family really."

"Doesn't he have any children?"

"Oh no – no, no," she replies with wide eyes, looking at me and pausing. "He did once. It was at the end of the war. He was in prison in Berlin at the time, because of the plot and all that. But I was here. Terrible, terrible. First the Russians took away all the men on the estate and," she makes a sweeping gesture with her arm, "just made them disappear. Never seen again. That was some time after they first arrived. They left the women and children at first – well, after they had had their way with them. But later, some months I think, when they found out that Heinrich's wife was of an old family, they came here, pulled his boys away from her, kicking and screaming, and dragged her

242

away. Later they took the boys too. I still remember the cries."

There is a long silence. Dust hangs in the air. I can still sense the grit inside me, itching incessantly. Then she continues.

"Heinrich was not allowed back here until the Wall fell. He knew they had probably been killed, but he didn't really know. He never asked me and I never told him. His patients – all those suffering people – I think they took the place of his family. He looked after them instead."

"But can't... isn't there anyone he could have asked about what happened to his wife and sons? How could he live like that, not knowing?"

"It was like that for so many people, Aydin. Children who lost their parents, parents who lost their children all through the war and afterwards... I don't know. The things people do to one another."

"Something similar happened to my parents," I say. "My grandparents were killed when my parents were small."

"Oh my God. You see? Poor dears. And how did they survive it?"

"They came to Germany, met, and had us," I reply. "They never talk about it either. They tried to start afresh. I only found out from my uncle the other day."

"Well, we can't blame them for not telling you. Some wounds are too deep."

She sighs. "It must have been even worse for the

people in Russia – what they did to their own people. Not that Russia was the only place. I mean, we did the same to our people and to the Jews, and, I don't know… every nation seems to have its shame. But here we are: we're alive," and she smiles and sniffs matter-of-factly.

Later I find Anton the butler and he says the count is feeling unwell and resting. He shows me to the guest room. It is painted blue and white and has dark green curtains and its own fireplace framed by hand-painted tiles; a new fire is dancing in the grate. Above the bed is a black-and-white photograph of a German army officer with far-receded hair and a confident, almost mischievous expression. There are two silver candle-sticks on the mantelpiece holding unlit candles; I light them from the flames of the fire. Outside the window I see the grounds strewn with mulch.

I try to lie on the bed but my legs are restless. I feel the magnet of drugs and the thought of drinking invades my head, as if from the faraway city. I just don't want that to come here, ever. I need to get on with something. I get up and go outside and find a rake in a shed around the back of the house, then start raking leaves into a large pile on the front lawn. It's hard work and the breeze takes some of the leaves off the heap and scatters them onto the snow on the drive.

After a good hour I have a great mound of leaves

and Anton comes out to watch me from the steps.

"Looking good," he calls, hands on hips. "I can see the grass again. There are bags around the back."

I fill three huge canvas bags and drag them to the shed. The house now has one green lawn among many brown ones and I'm exhausted. Yesterday's mist has lifted and there's a brooding cloud base from which tiny snowflakes are falling, swirling silently, coming to rest on everything.

Anton calls me for lunch. The two of us eat together with the cook in a simple dining room behind the kitchen. Mrs Schröder is quite short and sturdily built and has kind, inquisitive green eyes. Her permed hair is light grey; she must be in her mid-fifties.

"Welcome back," she says as she enters the room. Anton sits at the head of a long, rough-hewn wooden table and Mrs Schröder and I sit facing each other.

"There are only the two of us now," she confides. "This table was full of staff when you were last here."

"I'm surprised you remember me."

"Oh yes," she says, "we all remembered you."

"I'm sorry to hear about Count von Weser and the hospice."

"It's such a shame," she replies. "But I shan't leave. This is where I belong," and she glances at Anton, who eats in silence, looking down at his plate. "Anton too, no Anton?"

Anton makes an affirming sound.

"We get our board and lodging here and we get

some meaning from what we do. What more could you ask? Still, it's very sad, terribly sad; and to see all the patients going one by one."

"I heard that Peter died, the boy with leukaemia."

"Oh yes, Peter Rönpak. He used to light up this place. But then," she says, placing her hand on my arm, "I always preferred children. I think it should be a hospice for children."

We eat in silence for a while and I imagine a hospice full of boys and girls like Peter, sadness mingled with happiness.

"I came here to help but the count said he can't keep me because there's no money. But I don't really want money."

"Well, it will be a much happier place with you around. Right Anton?"

"Yes," he replies, glancing up from his plate.

"My father used to work for the von Wesers before the war," says Mrs Schröder, "looking after what was left of their horses. He died on the eastern front in 1944, God bless him. My mother says he was loyal to the von Wesers through thick and thin, so when Count Heinrich came back, I came to work here in his memory, and I never left." She laughs and looks contented. "The count's been pure goodness to me."

In the afternoon I rake the lawn on the other side of the main driveway so that things look symmetrical, by which time dusk is quite far advanced. As I finish I notice the count. He is standing like a ghost at the top of the steps looking out at me.

"Still here I see?" he says in a bright, weak voice. He is wearing a thick scarf and a Russian fur hat.

"Your garden needed raking," I reply, stopping in front of him and leaning on the rake. My breath is illuminated by the lamps on either side of the doorway.

"You'd better come in now," he says, turning away. His former erectness has gone out of him; he is bent over.

I bag the leaves in the last of the disappearing light and go indoors to do my prayers. Supper is with the staff; afterwards in bed I drop off quickly, but at around midnight I'm woken by the clanking of the window, blown by a gale. Treetops thunder and rush outside and gusts of sleet spatter the panes. My candles are down to their stumps and flickering in the draft. I blow them out, pull up my duvet and listen to the storm. Leaves and other debris are dashed against the window.

In the morning the snow that had been lying around the grounds is all but vanished; in its place are soggy leaves, twigs and the odd small branch. Looking to the left I see the two sections of lawn I had raked, covered with leaves again and looking only a slightly different shade from the others.

I join Anton and Mrs Schröder for breakfast. My whole body feels tired.

"Looks like my raking was for nothing."

"Never mind," says Mrs Schröder, smiling sympathetically at me and touching my hand. "Maybe you could work indoors today? You can help me in the kitchen, can't he Anton? And you can go and see the patients."

Later Anton takes me to the big, airy patients' lounge at the far end of the house. Its conservatory windows look out across the grounds. There are empty armchairs positioned alone and in groups, three small square tables with chairs around them, bookcases, and a television which is on but no sound comes from it, only the silent, grainy images of an old talk show. Facing it is a solitary old man slumped very low in his armchair with a tartan blanket draped across his bony knees; he is not watching the television, he is gazing somewhere beyond the horizon.

"Morning Mr Kühne, how are you today?" asks Anton, walking around into the man's line of sight. The old man's face stirs and he lifts his eyes and grey eyebrows.

"Morning, morning," he says absently.

"Would you like some tea, Mr Kühne?"

"What?" The old man frowns and cranes his head forward a little.

"Would you like some tea?"

"Oh, yes," he replies.

"Shall I go and make it?" I ask.

"Yes, but make a big pot, Ingrid always has tea," and he nods towards the back of the lounge, where an armchair faces away from us and out of the window.

When I return, I pour tea for Mr Kühne and pull up a little table for him. His hand shakes so much I'm afraid he might spill it but he doesn't want me to help him drink; he swats my hand away like a fly and otherwise ignores me. Then I go to Ingrid but she appears to be asleep. She is very small and withered and the armchair engulfs her. I arrange her tea on a table beside her and the clinking of the saucer wakes her; she looks at me momentarily. She has very sparse hair, twinkling eyes and creases radiating from their corners from a lifetime of smiling.

"Hello. And who are you?" she asks. Her voice is surprisingly strong and clear for such a small person.

"Aydin. Pleased to meet you," I say, and hold out my hand. She flaps off her blankets to liberate a thin, blotchy limb and we shake hands; she smiles a thousand wrinkles.

"I'm Ingrid."

"Yes, Anton told me."

"Aha," she says, "did he now? Well, aren't you going to sit down?"

I heave an armchair around to face her.

"Are you a new community service worker?"

"No, I'm just volunteering. I arrived yesterday."

"Volunteering? That's very brave. Everyone else's

left, but we soldier on."

"Yes," I laugh. "How come you're still here?"

"Me?" she laughs, placing her hand on her chest. "I've nowhere else to go."

"But didn't they move the others out to other hospices?"

"Move?" she says, frowning. "Oh no. I'm not going anywhere else. I like it here and it's near to my daughter's village. I'm going to die here. Why keep moving me around?"

I notice how warm the room is compared with the rest of the house. Ingrid has a thin face; her hair is dyed a chestnut brown to match her eyes but the die has half grown out and looks like tea-stains.

"Are you okay sitting here? You can't see much of anything."

"Well you can take me out for a walk if you like," she replies with a touch of pique. "But it's a mighty bother wrapping me up in enough clothes. They say I might catch pneumonia."

I take her out, mummified in coats, scarves and hats. We survey the work of the storm: it has taken down a large bough of a tree around the back of the house, leaving a gash in the trunk where it fell off. A pair of small birds hop around on the floored foliage, searching. Perhaps they have lost their nest.

15

I've been here on the estate for weeks. Nobody has acknowledged my continued presence or said anything about how long I might stay. I just work every day and everyone accepts it. I feel tired but settled and grateful.

Every afternoon I have coffee with the count, which I've come to look forward to. He tells me about the people he's known and the things he's seen and done. He tells me about the plot to kill Hitler and the government that was waiting in the wings, representatives in every foreign capital, and what happened to them all when it failed. The man in the picture above the fireplace in my room was the main instigator, he says. And he tells me about his childhood, riding horses, playing with Bismarck's grandchildren, sailing on the Baltic.

The grit has mostly gone now. I wish Steffi was here with me now so I could share what is happening to me; so she could see she was right for me to come. My body's strong again from all the work. Every time drug-thoughts creep up on me, I get up and do something – even in the night, when I go to the kitchen and wash up or clean. Mrs Schröder says there's a friendly elf in the house.

I eat my meals with her and Anton, and every few days I go up to see Countess Carla. It's because of her that I'm standing here now on the front steps with Anton, waiting for my parents and Uncle Mejid to arrive. "How could you not invite them?" she said. "You must invite them! Think of what they've been through, think of what they've lost. Now you must make sure they know they're not losing you, hiding out here in the depths of Brandenburg!"

There they are in the distance, trundling slowly up the drive in Uncle Mejid's car. I'm nervous about what the people here will think, and about what my family will think. Our worlds are so different.

My father and I stand in a long embrace, then I hug and kiss my mother, who keeps looking at me as if she's seen something new in me. They shake hands shyly with Anton. Uncle Mejid embraces me, grinning broadly.

"We've brought something," says my father, opening the boot. "Your mother's made a few things."

That can only be one thing: food, and lots of it.

Anton and I carry three large cool boxes up the steps and into the house. Then my parents, my uncle and I sit in the reception room and wait in silence. They're smiling, which is good.

Count von Weser comes in, dressed in the same tweed jacket he wore at the prison the first time I saw him. He's gained weight since I've been here and it almost fits him again.

"Heinrich von Weser," he says, his voice alert and warm, and he shakes their hands and falls into his feather armchair with a thump.

"May I begin by saying that Aydin has got us back on our feet again here singlehandedly?"

"Oh," says my father, clearly pleased and a bit confused, like me.

"Yes," says von Weser. "I'm not exaggerating. He came here unannounced and insisted on staying, and he hasn't stopped working for a single minute, and with such determination."

My parents shift forwards to the edges of their chairs, transfixed. Uncle Mejid is smiling.

"He's kept the grounds clean, prepared a vegetable plot for the spring, he gets up early, he spends every morning with the patients." I blush while von Weser lists my activities. "He keeps my other staff from abandoning me, and he visits my ancient aunt and talks to her twice a week, which is more than anyone else. If he hadn't come when he did, we would have gone under. I'm afraid I've been rather unwell."

My mother and father are starting to glow with pride, looking at von Weser and glancing over at me.

"Best of all," continues the old man, leaning forward and clasping his hands around his knee, "he doesn't mind spending half an hour with me every day so I can regale him with tales of the past."

I intercept him: "No! That's... it's me who's benefiting. I was a wreck when I came here. And you wouldn't believe all the things Count von Weser's done in his life."

Then I think suddenly of my parents' sad and secret past. Only Uncle Mejid knows that I know.

"And," resumes von Weser, "he pays his dues to God more than all of us put together. It's been quite a reminder for me."

What? My mind races and I blush even more. He must mean my prayers; but I thought I'd kept that secret.

"Really?" says my mother, genuinely surprised. It's the first thing she's said. "He prays?"

"Yes. I've seen my own situation very differently of late, and it's because of your son," replies von Weser. "His prayers reminded me."

I rummage hurriedly through my memories. Maybe Anton walked in on me once when I was praying.

"We're so grateful you've taken Aydin in," says my mother. "I can see he's found his place here."

That's the first good thing my mother's said about me in a long time. I wish I could tell her I know about her parents being killed, but it would expose Uncle Mejid, who's leaning back with knowing, moist, victorious eyes.

Anton enters and says something quietly to the count, who looks up at him, says yes, nods, and Anton leaves.

"I'm told you came bearing gifts," he says. "Perhaps Aydin can give you a tour of the estate, then we can meet in an hour for a Turkish banquet?"

I show my family the grounds and most of the house, including my room, where a towel is spread on the floor at an angle as a prayer mat. That must be how Anton knows. I scoop it up while they're not looking and toss it onto the bed.

Later we make our way to the dining room where my mother's food has been arrayed in dishes on the sideboard. There is an enormous amount of it. All three of us exclaim with delight when we see it spread out so beautifully. Roasted red peppers, sizzling and spitting on a hot platter. Minced meat on skewers with green peppers between. Beans, orange, white and brown. Grilled aubergine puree with chopped coriander sprinkled over. Meatballs. Twenty or thirty lamb chops. Great wads of flatbread, probably from the shop around the corner from their flat. It's the only thing my mother doesn't make herself.

"Please lead the way and help yourselves," announces the count from behind us as he enters, ushering us in front of him. Then Anton appears with Aunt Carla on his arm, walking slowly. He seats her carefully at one end of the table, then queues behind us. I've never seen her downstairs before.

Once we're all seated, von Weser looks around at us.

"May I introduce to you my dear aunt, Carla? She has kept this house safe for us for nearly eighty years."

"And these are my parents," I tell her, "and my uncle Mejid."

"I am so pleased to meet you," she declares. "You must be enormously proud of your son. He's made such a difference to us here."

Von Weser gestures to the food in front of us. "Our first Turkish meal at the house and we shall never forget it. A generous feast to brighten our straightened circumstances."

Then he picks up his cutlery and looks at me expectantly.

"Aydin?"

"Bismillah," I say, picking up my knife and fork to begin.

"Countess Carla said I should invite you," I say to my family.

"Yes," responds Carla in her clear voice. "I did. I call your son Aydin the Conqueror. Such a fighter!" She shakes her fist like before. "So, now we have the honour of dining with a sultan's parents."

My parents glance at each other; Uncle Mejid keeps his eyes to himself.

Later, when we're saying goodbye at the steps, my uncle takes both of von Weser's hands and shakes them, beaming but saying nothing. My father embraces the old man briefly. My mother thanks von Weser, and although they don't embrace or even shake hands, they stand facing each other for a long time.

Then my father produces an envelope and hands it to me.

"This came for you. It's from Serbia of all places. Do you know who it could be from?"

"No idea," I reply.

There's only one Serbian I know, and he's dead. I take the letter quickly.

"I'll open it later."

After another round of goodbyes, their car trundles away down the drive. I already miss them.

I'm in my room late in the evening. The envelope is sitting on the mantelpiece, begging to be opened. This has to be about Slobodan, but who would have found my parents' address?

Standing at the fireplace, I take the letter, slide my finger beneath the crackling gum and pull out a small piece of paper folded in half.

"Dear Aydin,
I am not dead."

I move to my bed and sit, blinking blankly at the spidery words. In the top right corner it just says "Serbia" and a date three weeks ago, written in my friend's scrawled hand.

"After I saw you in hospital," it goes on, "I was angry for what they did to you, so I took revenge. It is the Serbian way. I finished off Zola and Lok. The world is a better place. But I had to leave Germany because of it. Don't come and look for me. I'm starting a new life. You should do the same.

Thinking of old times.

Slobodan"

My candles flicker in the draft. Slobodan shot Zola. Slobodan killed Lok. Slobodan executed Steffi's dad. Slobodan did away with my tormentors. I wonder whether I ought to feel angry for her or happy for myself. But as the news sinks in, I feel safe, I feel grateful. I feel a great weight lifting off my shoulders. I feel only a bit afraid of what it means for Steffi. My best friend killed her dad. Not that I'd tell her – no way. Never.

Steffi. I want to see her. I head down to von Weser's little office and phone her.

"Hello?"

"Steffi, it's Aydin."

"Aydin!" she gasps. "I thought you'd never call.

Where are you?"

"I'm at that hospice. I did what you said. It was the right thing."

"I know, Aydin."

I go silent for a while. I can hear her breathing. I'm full of things I want to say to her.

"Steffi, I... I want to invite you here for the day. I want to see you."

"I'd love to see you too, Aydin."

"Yeah?" I smile. "When?"

"Next week?"

I give her the address.

That night I don't sleep much. I keep thinking it all through. Slobodan – Slobodan who seemed so washed up and hopeless – Slobodan who they thought was suicidal – Slobodan went straight out and shot Zola and the Master. It's hard to get my head around. Did he do that just for me? True, those two men had been bad to me, but I did walk right into their world. Then I remember what Wolfgang said; maybe Slobodan wanted to make up for something else in the past.

My mind gets lost in speculations and I sink slowly into a turbulent sleep. I'm on Kurfürstendamm again, holding a steel bar in my sleeve. Slobodan's there. Zola's there. Yez the Kurd is there. The Master arrives and Slobodan shoots them all but they don't die or even do anything, they just stand around talking strangely, which is when I know I'm dreaming. Then Steffi comes. She isn't all made-up, she's like she was when I visited her. I'm about to bury my head in her shoulder to escape the whole thing, but I don't. I hold back. This is a dream, I say to myself, and I look indifferently, coldly even, at Zola and the Master and Yez and Slobodan.

Then I decide to wake up on my own terms.

16

Steffi is coming. She's arriving at the station I arrived at that freezing day, months ago. Sitting in the ticket kiosk is the same man, reading his tabloid through thick glasses. I wonder what they had here in the East before tabloids.

I run up the wide, worn stone steps to the platform. The railway tracks converge into the distance beneath an avenue of trees which were bare when I arrived; now they're bursting with buds and birds. Tiny seeds float in shafts of sunlight.

The train arrives and comes to a slow, screeching halt. Steffi steps down further along the platform, wearing a bleached denim jacket and carrying a small leather bag slung over her shoulder on a long strap. We beam at each other as she approaches; the May sun warms my face. There is a bounce in her walk. From the eaves of the station canopy comes the chirping of hungry chicks whose mother swoops in. We embrace and I feel the beating of her heart and inhale her perfume.

"Let's go," I say, "the car's outside, I want to take you somewhere."

We drive out of the little town along the road I walked on last winter. I watch her face from out of the corner of my eye, drinking in her presence. We turn down a side road, then another; it doesn't take me long to find the spot I rowed from on my winter walk. The same boat has been returned to its mooring. We step carefully aboard its creaking planks and I push it out onto the glass with an oar.

I row slowly, facing her.

"You look so well," she says, her eyes twinkling as she examines me.

"You too."

The air is completely still, the temperature the same as my skin.

"It's so lovely here," she says, looking around. "I've never been out in Brandenburg before."

Some waterbirds chatter far off. Soon the lake narrows and the water's flow becomes noticeable. The waiting willow whose fingers had looked so forlorn and disappointed in the winter is now a pale green veil, its slender leaves kissing the water's liquid mirror, danced on by mayflies.

"This whole place has been so good for me."

"I told you," she says, smiling and trailing her hand in the water, making a soft little wake that intertwines with the boat's trail.

There is a heavy splash somewhere and we catch sight of widening rings. A duck fusses as she emerges from foliage at the water's edge followed by seven fluffy ducklings and a laggard eighth, making us laugh.

"And you?" I ask. I pause, wondering how best to put it. "Are you alright?"

"Yeah," she exhales, looking away. She looks down, then at the riverbank. "I feel quite sad a lot of the time. I still kind of loved my dad, despite everything."

The boat is slipping along quicker now; I barely need to pull the oars.

"I do think about his killer," she says – and I wonder with a jolt what makes her bring him up like that, whether she somehow knows.

"He did me a favour, in a horrible way, because I would have never escaped."

I picture Slobodan, somewhere in the arid Balkans. I wish he could see us here.

"Before my father got into what he got into," she continues, "he taught karate to so many people – children, adults, boys, girls – he was good at what he did."

I ship the oars as the current takes a proper hold of the boat.

"There were things he would never talk about," she continues. "His childhood. He put the anger inside him into his sport." She looks across at the far bank. "If only he'd kept it that way."

She looks at me for a moment, first at my face, then at the outline of my head and my scars. We pass beneath an oak's bough, its verdant main arm and smaller limbs extending across the river, hungry new leaves reaching and probing.

"Are you going to stay out here?" she asks.

"Yeah," I say. "If I can."

She looks at the dark, reedy bank as it slides by. I watch the side of her face but it is inscrutable; a cradle of things I may never know.

She looks back at me evenly.

"Good."

"You think so?"

"Yes."

I smile at her. I want to tell her to stay here with me and never go away.

She surveys me with a knowing smile.

I'll take her back to the house later and introduce her to the count. I'll show her around, show her the patients, then take her up to Countess Carla, who'll say something priceless.

We might eat with Anton and Mrs Schröder. If we're lucky we'll eat with the count. And if we do, there's another idea I want to float. I want us to start taking on more patients again. Not old people. Children, like

Peter Rönpak. I think he'll say yes, now that he knows I'm sticking around, now that he's a bit stronger. And I want to recruit volunteers too, but from the local town this time, not from prisons. Or, maybe even from there. Maybe there are other Aydins in there.

And I want Steffi to come back and stay. But I won't ask her now; it seems too soon.

For now, I just let the boat slip on down the river as it widens into a lake. I let it glide, slide, until it gradually comes to rest, lazily askew, far from the banks.

I turn and lean back into Steffi's lap and look up at the warm and cloudless sky and listen to the buzzing insects, the birds, and all the sounds of the coming summer.